10% $^{12}/_{15}$
10-16

LO

FORTHCOMING BY C. S. CHALLINOR

Murder in the Raw

A Rex Graves Mystery

CHRISTMAS IS
MURDER

C.S. Challinor

MIDNIGHT INK
WOODBURY, MINNESOTA

First Edition
Second Printing, 2008

Book design and format by Donna Burch
Cover design by Gavin Dayton Duffy
Cover art holly © Photodisc
Editing by Connie Hill

Midnight Ink, an imprint of Llewellyn Publications

Library of Congress Cataloging-in-Publication Data
Challinor, C. S. (Caroline).
   Christmas is murder : a Rex Graves mystery / C. S. Challinor. — 1st ed.
      p.   cm.
   ISBN 978-0-7387-1359-5
   I. Title.
PS3603.H3366C47   2008
813'.6—dc22   2008010937

Midnight Ink
Llewellyn Publications
2143 Wooddale Drive, Dept. 978-0-7387-1359-5
Woodbury, MN 55125-2989 USA
www.midnightinkbooks.com

Printed in the United States of America

CAST OF CHARACTERS

IN ORDER OF APPEARANCE

HOTEL STAFF

DAHLIA SMITHINGS, hotel proprietor who lost her son in Iraq.

SANDY BELLOWS, head cook with more to her than meets the eye.

ROSIE PORTER, ambitious waitress with an axe to grind.

CLIFFORD BEADEL, odd-job man suspected of a past murder.

GUESTS

REX GRAVES, sleuth—a Scottish Barrister revisiting a childhood haunt.

HENRY D. LAWDRY, disabled WWII veteran of wealthy means.

MIRIAM GREENBAUM, New York literary agent attending a book fair in Brighton.

WANDA MARTYR, recent divorcee with a penchant for snooping.

HELEN D'ARCY, friend of the above who falls for the intrepid sleuth.

ANTHONY SMART, antiques dealer with designs on the hotel.

PATRICK VANCE, Smart's gay partner, an odd duck of artistic temperament.

YVETTE & CHARLEY PERKINS, young newlyweds hiding a secret.

PROLOGUE

Mrs. D. Smithings requests the pleasure of
the company of Reginald Graves, QC
at Swanmere Manor, December 23 to 27.
RSVP

REX REREAD THE CARD before thrusting it into his coat pocket in preparation for his trip, wondering again at the formal nature of the invitation. After all, Dahlia Smithings and his mother were old friends, and he had visited Swanmere Manor as a boy. Not in his wildest dreams could he imagine the place converted into a hotel. Still, he might encounter some interesting guests there and anything was better than staying home alone over Christmas. His mother was visiting a sick friend in Perth, and his significant other had left on a humanitarian mission to Iraq—three weeks ago now, and still not a word.

Surveying the suitcase gaping on the bed, Rex decided he'd packed enough warm clothes for a week in the south of England.

Here in Edinburgh it was four degrees Celsius, with a chance of evening showers and a forecast of plunging temperatures. "Lucky wee beggar," he muttered, thinking of his son in sunny Florida on a student exchange program.

Before he opened the front door he ran through a mental checklist: cell phone, wallet, car keys, supply of Clan tobacco, Sudoku puzzles. Then, after squeezing into his brand-new Mini Cooper in the dark and the drizzle, he set out for Waverley Station to catch the overnight train down to London.

ONE

SANDY BELLOWS BLITHELY DICED away at onions on a wooden chopping board, her rolled-up sleeves revealing freckled forearms the size of hams. "Can you believe it? Snow. And us so near the sea. Another twelve inches tomorrow, they said on the radio."

With a shrug of her voluptuous shoulders, Rosie picked up the laden tea tray from the counter. "You can never rely on what the weatherman says."

"Polly in the village told me her husband found an old man by the side of the road. Stiff as a board he was with hypothermia. Another load of snow and there'll be no getting in or out of the hotel," Sandy Bellows pursued.

"Cook, what's this I hear about more snow?" Mrs. Smithings asked, darting into the kitchen, a gaunt apparition in black, with pearls encircling her high lace collar.

"Another foot tomorrow," Mrs. Bellows repeated. "Just in time for Christmas Eve."

"Hurry along with that tray, Rosie," Mrs. Smithings commanded the young girl. "It's four thirty."

As Rosie left the kitchen, Dahlia Smithings gazed out of the frost-encrusted window, her profile with the white chignon as austere as those found on Roman coins. "Some of our guests are due to leave tomorrow if the snow clears," she mused aloud. "I do wish the American was one of them."

"She can be quite trying from what I hear," the cook agreed. "The others are pleasant enough, though. Like that gay couple, Mr. Smart and Mr. Vance. Nicely mannered they are. And that old gent with one arm. I wonder what his story is, alone at Christmas, and him such a—"

"Yes, yes, Cook. Enough gossip. We have dinner to prepare. Where's Clifford?"

"Chopping wood."

"Tell him to stockpile logs in the cellar in case we're unable to access the woodshed over the next few days."

"You expect it'll get that bad?"

"Louise was unable to come in today from the village. Imagine what it will be like tomorrow if this keeps up." Mrs. Smithings stared thoughtfully at the sheets of snow falling slantways from the sky. "Mr. Graves is supposed to be arriving tomorrow from Edinburgh—he may have to cancel his reservation. Well, call Clifford in," she told Mrs. Bellows. "We need him here in the kitchen."

"Not much use he'll be," the cook muttered, wiping her hands on her apron. She ambled over to the scullery door and called Clifford.

"Tea ready?" the wizened old man asked with glee, depositing his axe on the floor.

"We need you to help with dinner."

"Me?"

"Can you peel potatoes?" Mrs. Smithings asked impatiently.

"Wot? Wi' these gnarled ould 'ands?" He pulled off his mittens to display two arthritic extremities. "Eh can 'ardly chop wood."

The cook handed him a vegetable parer. Grumbling, Clifford eased himself onto a chair at the pine table in front of a mound of potatoes. "Mind you get all the eyes out," she directed.

"Me 'ands be so bleedin' cold they can 'ardly hold the bleedin' taters."

"Watch your tongue, old man," admonished Mrs. Smithings as she swept regally from the kitchen.

Clifford's reply was cut short by Rosie, returning with her empty tray. "Here, give me that," she said, snatching the parer out of his hand, and she began to peel a potato with vigor.

"Wot about my tea then?" Clifford asked, jerking his head over his shoulder at Cook.

"I'll put the kettle on. I need a bit of a breather myself," she said.

A sly grin spread over Clifford's etched face. "While the cat's away ... Where's her ladyship anyways?" he asked Rosie.

"Probably in her office."

"She'll be gone awhile then, allus lookin' at them photos, she is."

"How do you know she looks at photos?"

"I sees her sometimes through the window when I clips the hedge. Just stares at them, she does. Anything to go wi' the tea?" he asked the cook. "Me stomach's growlin' like a bear in a cage."

"I kept some iced almond tarts back."

"Ouch!" Rosie, who had nicked herself with the parer, watched transfixed as a bulb of blood grew on her thumb.

Clifford gave a wheezy laugh. "Y'aren't much better at it than me. Best get something for that afore you bleed all over the place. If the guests saw that in their food, they'd feel swimey, like as not."

———

The guests, all but the honeymooners, flocked around the tea items set out on lace doilies on the Victorian table. A Christmas tree decked in silver bells and burgundy bows twinkled with fairy lights in a corner of the drawing room.

Anthony Smart, upon extricating a cup of tea from the table, commandeered a wing armchair by the fire. Late thirties and balding, with a close-trimmed beard, he wore designer spectacles and an obsidian signet ring. Stretching his long legs before him, he gazed in appreciation at the white-painted wood trelliswork surrounding the fireplace. "Webb," he said knowingly to a charming blonde taking her seat on one of the sofas.

"Webb?" she asked, balancing a small plate on her lap while she stirred her tea, her blue eyes as bright as the sequins adorning the neck of her sweater.

"The fireplace designer," Anthony explained.

"Oh, really?" Helen d'Arcy looked about the room, taking in the velvet curtains and soft furnishings in navy and cream, matching the vine and flower motif carpet. "The manor probably hasn't changed much since 1898. But I daresay you'd know more about that, Anthony—being an interior decorator."

"I'd guess Morris and Company did the design," Smart agreed. "Such variety of pattern and color is their hallmark, after all."

"I just adore this hunting scene," interrupted an American voice. Miriam Greenbaum planted herself in front of the fireplace and peered over her thick-rimmed glasses at the oil painting above it. "Worth megabucks, I'll bet."

"No doubt," Anthony concurred, his frown evidencing displeasure at the substantial figure in plum velour invading his space.

"Probably been in the Smithings family for generations."

Anthony tapped the air with the toe of his polished shoe. "So, how did you find out about Swanmere Manor Hotel?" he asked the American woman. "It's hardly well advertised."

"Stroke of luck," she replied. "A contact from the Brighton Book Festival told me about it."

"Excuse me." Patrick Vance daintily stepped around the literary agent to sit opposite Anthony, while a pert, fortyish brunette made herself comfortable beside Helen.

"Feeling better, Sleeping Beauty?" Anthony asked the new arrival.

"Much," Wanda Martyr replied.

"Good. You need plenty of rest after the ordeal you've been through," Helen soothed her friend.

"Aren't these almond tarts to die for?" Wanda said, brushing crumbs from penciled lips.

Helen licked the icing off her fork. "Mm. Fabulous."

"What are you sketching?" Wanda asked Patrick, who had propped a pad against one knee.

"I'm just doodling." A pale lock of hair fell across his smooth brow.

"Don't believe it for a minute," Anthony said. "Patrick doesn't doodle. He never misses a detail, do you, Patrick? That's what makes him so in demand with our clients."

"This is just relaxation. I'm drawing the Christmas tree with the three of you in the foreground."

"You might want to take a stab at me sometime," Miriam Greenbaum butted in, sinking into an empty sofa. "It would make a great souvenir to take back to the States."

Patrick mumbled something noncommittal in response. At that moment, querulous tones arose from the far side of the room. "Urgh, I mistook the coffee for tea," an old man complained, half rising from his armchair with the aid of his good arm.

Anthony put out a hand. "Don't disturb yourself, Mr. Lawdry. I'm going that way for a refill. I'd be happy to bring you some tea."

"Call me Henry. And most obliged."

"One lump or two?" Anthony called from the table.

"Two, please. I confess to having a sweet tooth, which is why I wear dentures now, I suppose."

"Sugar is poison," Anthony agreed. "It wreaks havoc on the body cells, causing premature aging."

The two women friends on the sofa suddenly came to from their private conversation.

"No!" Wanda exclaimed.

Anthony paused on his way back to Lawdry, two cups in hand. "There must be thirty grams of sugar in those iced tarts," he said, nodding at Wanda's plate.

"Nonsense," Miriam Greenbaum intervened. "It's fat that's the killer. I know something about nutrition. Most of the nonfiction books I represent are on diet."

"Believe me," Patrick said, looking up from his sketchpad, "what Anthony doesn't know about health isn't worth knowing."

Just then, a gasp sounded from across the room, and they all turned to look. The old man was having a seizure. Patrick reached him first.

"Was it the sugar or the fat content?" Anthony asked wryly, pointing to the fallen pastry at the old man's feet. "He is going to be okay, isn't he?"

Wanda set down her plate with a shaky hand. "Well, I ate two tarts and I feel perfectly all right."

"Me too," Helen said. "Well, just one, actually. That's my limit."

"Mr. Lawdry? Henry?" Patrick questioned urgently. "He's unconscious. Quick, get Charley Perkins from the honeymoon suite. He's a paramedic. Tell him it might be a heart attack."

Anthony rushed from the room while the three women hovered around the afflicted man's chair.

"Poor old thing," Helen commiserated. "He's gone very pale. Is that white icing he choked up?"

Wanda stared in horror, hand on her throat. Miriam Greenbaum suggested they get hold of the management.

"I'll go," Patrick offered, and left the room.

On the stairs outside the drawing room, a Cockney voice asked, "What did Henry eat before he got taken poorly?"

"Coffee and a tart," Anthony answered. "I hope you can do something, Charley."

The next second, Charley Perkins came dashing barefoot into the drawing room, shirttail half hanging out of his trousers. "Maybe something didn't agree with his medication," he said when he saw Lawdry. He leaned over and began checking the old man's vitals conscientiously.

"Perhaps we should call an ambulance," Helen suggested.

Charley straightened up and shook his head sadly. "Too late for that—he's gone."

Wanda gasped.

"Could it have been food poisoning?" Ms. Greenbaum demanded.

"Food poisoning?" Dahlia Smithings railed behind them. "In my establishment? Impossible!"

———

By six o'clock, Lawdry's body had been carried up to his room, upon Mrs. Smithings' instructions, and his death reported to the local authorities, who apologized that it would be awhile until anyone could reach the hotel due to the snow.

"Leave the window open to preserve the body," the doctor told her over the phone. "We should be able to get to it in a day or two."

"But the day after tomorrow will be Christmas Eve! I have guests staying, and one more expected tomorrow by train. An eminent QC from Scotland and friend of the family."

The doctor mumbled his regrets and left Mrs. Smithings pondering the now-silent phone.

"What are we going to do?" Rosie asked, stepping into the back parlor that served as Mrs. Smithings' office.

"Do? Continue as before," exhorted the hotel owner. "Serve the guests more tea. Where are they?"

"In the drawing room, ma'am. If we go on at this rate, we'll run out of tea."

"Well, offer them sherry then. Even though it is not strictly Christmas yet, it might be appropriate under the circumstances."

Rosie returned to the drawing room where she produced a cut-glass decanter of sherry from an armoire.

"Special occasion, Rosie?" Anthony asked, eying the decanter from his armchair.

"Mrs. Smithings doesn't usually bring out the sherry until Christmas Eve, but she thought it might calm our nerves. I'll be right back with some glasses."

"What an eccentric old bird that Dahlia Smithings is," Ms. Greenbaum observed, prodding her BlackBerry. "*Almost total Prohibition is practiced at this hotel,*" she typed to her assistant in New York. "*Sherry is served only at Christmas—or if somebody dies. All they drink is hot tea, a vile concoction, and I can't even get to a pub, what with all this blasted snow!*"

"I still can't get over poor Henry's death," Helen announced to the room.

Her friend Wanda shivered. "Imagine us staying here with a dead body upstairs."

"There's no helping it," Helen said. "Swanmere Manor is two miles uphill from the village and sixteen miles from the nearest town. The country lanes will be impenetrable until a snow plough can come to the rescue. What a dreadful time to pass away!"

Yvette Perkins, who had joined them and was sitting hand in hand with Charley on the loveseat, dabbed her nose with a handkerchief. "Henry told me he lost his wife last February. His daughter died years ago and his son emigrated to Australia. He came to Swanmere Manor so he'd have company at Christmas."

"That is so sad," Helen exclaimed. "I hope this doesn't put a damper on your honeymoon."

"Well, I'm not going to let it spoil things." Yvette tucked a strand of bleached hair behind her ear. "I mean, this was a wedding present from my mum. She chose this hotel because it's quiet and has really good home-cooked food."

Helen and Wanda murmured assent.

"It'll be a hard act to follow," Yvette continued. "I hope Charley here doesn't expect me to cook him four square meals a day."

"No, but I expect other favours four times a day."

"Oh, he's a bad one!" Yvette chided with a blush while the others laughed—until they remembered poor Henry Lawdry upstairs and grew sober-faced again.

"Funny to think you're here celebrating your wedding while I'm celebrating my divorce," Wanda observed.

"Oh, I didn't know," Yvette said. "I'm so sorry."

"Don't be. He was a wanker." Wanda appraised Charley. "But I think you have a keeper here, love."

The newlyweds squeezed hands. "Oh, I think so," Yvette said.

Rosie reappeared carrying glasses the size of thimbles and began dispensing sherry. "I'm sorry dinner will be a bit delayed this evening owing to the circumstances," she faltered, serving the women first.

"What quaint little tumblers," Miriam Greenbaum hooted. "No danger of us letting our hair down, is there?"

"Just as well," Anthony replied, patting his bald pate.

14

"Don't mind if I do," Patrick said, accepting a glass from Rosie. "What are you busy working on, Miriam?"

The literary agent rooted around in a big box file. "*A President for Our Time: A Biography of George W. Bush*," she replied, pulling out a hefty manuscript.

"Must be fiction," Anthony quipped.

"Ah, now, I won't be drawn into a political discussion with you, Anthony."

"Anthony," he corrected, placing the emphasis on the 't'. "The 'h' is silent in the English pronunciation of the name."

"Anthony is very particular about these things," Patrick hurriedly explained.

"Well, it *is* my name and I object to Yanks coming along and corrupting every word in the English language. Not to mention—"

Miriam Greenbaum opened her mouth to speak.

"Er-um, I'll go and get a progress report on dinner," Rosie murmured as she finished making the sherry round.

"Oh, wonderful," Helen said. "I'm starving. Are you, Wanda?"

"Well, they do say funerals make you hungry."

"This is a bit like a funeral," Yvette agreed. "Us sitting around all formal and sipping sherry."

Wanda Martyr turned to Charley. "Do you think Henry might have choked on his dentures? He said they were always coming loose."

"Unlikely. However, he was taking medication for a weak heart."

"Charley was advising Henry on his medications," Yvette said proudly.

"Well, not advising, exactly," her husband corrected, "but he did discuss his condition with me."

"Mercifully, it was quick," Anthony said.

Miriam Greenbaum glanced up from her manuscript. "Until the proper authorities get here, I guess we won't know exactly what happened. Someone could have murdered the poor old guy, for all we know."

"What makes you think that?" Anthony demanded.

"It would be pretty easy. I happen to rep some of the best mystery writers in the business, so I'm something of an expert. I bet I could commit the perfect murder and get away with it."

Rosie returned at that moment to summon the guests into dinner.

Patrick set aside his sketchpad. "I hope you're wrong about the food poisoning, Miriam. I've got a very delicate stomach."

"*E. coli* or *salmonella* could have crept into the kitchen," Anthony supposed aloud.

Miriam rose from the sofa with an indulgent smile. "Oh, how you do fuss, Anthony!"

Anthony Smart stared daggers at the American's back. "Why couldn't it have been her instead of Henry?" he murmured to his partner as they followed the others to dinner.

TWO

HUFFING AND PUFFING UP the gently sloping hill in the snow on tennis racquets laced to his boots, Rex caught his first glimpse of Swanmere Manor after almost forty years. The steep-pitched roofs with verge board trim bristled with chimneys, crushed beneath the weight of the leaden sky.

He remembered the house only vaguely from when he'd visited as a child, before the Smithings fell on hard times and turned it into a hotel. The late Colonel Smithings had made unwise investments in the Far East, forcing the couple to take in paying guests, though Mrs. Smithings drew the line at actually advertising her establishment. Reservations were by invitation only—once she had made the necessary inquiries. Nobody off the street was permitted to stay, and consequently, there was not as much as a sign at the driveway entrance.

The invitation rested in his trench coat pocket where he had placed it the day before. No matter that Mrs. Smithings and his mother had gone to boarding school together and their husbands had served in India at the same time: Dahlia Smithings was a stickler for formality. In his other pocket snuggled a half-grown, white-and-tan puppy that he'd found whimpering in the snow by the station. Other than weighing down his coat on that side, the dog proved no trouble. Rex had no idea what he was going to do with it.

As he passed through the tall, wrought-iron gates, he fancied he recognized the dormer window of the attic room where he'd spent a childhood summer. Coiffed with snow, it peered blearily from above the board-and-batten siding of the second story. Bereft of their leaves, climbing vines clung to the red brick as though for warmth, the circular driveway that once welcomed visitors to the stone porch buried beneath the snow. Only the smoke billowing from the chimneys gave any sign of habitation, and yet Mrs. Smithings had said there would be a half-dozen guests for Christmas dinner.

Tramping across the white-carpeted lawn on the pair of racquets, a suitcase skating behind him at the end of his belt, Rex watched as the front door opened and a figure in black stepped onto the porch.

"Reginald, my dear, you got here after all," Dahlia Smithings cawed across the driveway. "I would have recognized you anywhere with that shock of red hair, but my, how you have grown! Last time I saw you, you were in boy's shorts with your socks constantly escaping your garters," she said as he reached the porch. "I trust your mother is well?"

Rex winced inwardly at the vision of himself as a lad. He had indeed been an untidy-looking child, his mother attempting to anticipate his gargantuan growth spurts by buying him oversize clothes. Down to his last breath, he barely managed to gasp a greeting in reply as icy flakes stung his cheeks. Just a few more steps and he would finally, *finally* arrive.

"What on earth are those contraptions on your feet?" Mrs. Smithings asked. "Oh, I must say, how very resourceful of you. You must have trekked the two miles from the station."

"I was hoping to play tennis while I was here," Rex explained haltingly, recovering his breath on the doorstep. "I remembered playing on the lawn court. I never anticipated all this snow."

So far, Mrs. Smithings had not noticed the puppy whose black muzzle peeked from his coat pocket, and Rex decided it was just as well, certain there was a no pets policy at the hotel.

"No, the snow is most unusual," she agreed. "The weather is going to the dogs, just like everything else in this country. Cliff-ORD! Where is that beastly man when I need him? Clifford, there you are. Take this gentleman's suitcase up to the green paisley room."

Rex's gaze landed upon an old man in tattered tweed whose face looked as though it had been hewn out of bark.

"Wot, carry it up all them stairs?" Clifford asked Mrs. Smithings, cupping his ear as if he couldn't be hearing correctly.

"Do you have a better idea how to get it up there?"

He stared hard at Rex unstrapping his makeshift snowshoes, clearly trying to convey to his employer that the new guest was three times his strength and size, and she must be blind and half-witted not to notice.

"Clifford, you are worse than useless. Then perhaps you can carry the racquets and that bag he has over his shoulder." Mrs. Smithings closed the front door and addressed Rex. "Whatever you do, don't tip him like our American guest does. That will only encourage his idleness. I will show you your room. Tea is at four-thirty in the drawing room. Do you recall where that is?"

Rex glanced past the staircase to the end of a passage to his right where a set of French doors stood open, releasing the sound of desultory chatter.

"Aye, not much seems to have changed since I was a lad." Except that the manor had shrunk and wore a stiff and outmoded look, he thought.

"Well, Clifford, as you can see, is immensely changed in that he is more useless than ever. I only keep him on because he has been with the family so long, and his father before him."

Clifford trailed behind them up the stairs, Mrs. Smithings leading the way. Rex wondered if Clifford's feelings had been hurt by her insensitive remarks, but fortunately, the old man didn't appear to hear very well.

"There have been changes made upstairs," she continued. "We added bathrooms. All the suites are taken, but as Mr. Lawdry is no longer with us, you will have the men's bathroom to yourself. Rosie put a pile of fresh towels in there for your use."

The staircase angled to the left upon a short gallery, then left again, climbing to a first-story landing, which forked in opposite directions. Mrs. Smithings led Rex to his room in the west wing.

"This will do me fine," Rex said, glancing around at the Victorian furniture and hand-stitched quilt embracing a brass four-poster bed. The window overlooked the driveway, the impressions made in the snow by his racquets already losing definition as flakes white and chaste as communion wafers floated down past the panes and superimposed their predecessors on the ground below.

Even as he watched, the flurries thickened and picked up a furious pace.

"The heating is on," Mrs. Smithings said behind him, "but you may light the fire in the grate if you wish. Thank you, Clifford. Now go and ask Cook if she needs your dubious help in the kitchen."

She waited until Clifford was out of earshot and then turned to Rex. "I'm afraid we lost one of our guests," she told him. "A Mr. Henry Lawdry."

"Lost him?" Rex asked, imagining him having taken a wrong turn somewhere on the estate and disappearing into a snowdrift.

"He died yesterday afternoon, of a stroke, apparently. He was very old. I thought I should mention it before one of the guests does. We called an ambulance but no one could get here. So I have locked him in room number four, next door, with the window wide open to preserve the body until someone can attend to it."

"How are the guests taking it?"

"They are a trifle upset. He was a popular old gentleman, a decorated veteran." Mrs. Smithings turned on a table lamp, dispelling the winter gloom. "We now have eight guests including yourself: Charles and Yvette Perkins, the newlyweds; two men from London in the interior design business; two ladies from Derbyshire holidaying together; and a New York literary agent by the name of Miriam Greenbaum. I shall make the formal introductions at tea."

She paused, gazing at Rex with a faraway look in her faded blue eyes. He wondered if she was remembering her son killed on active duty in Basra two years before. Rex had not seen him since he was last here, and hadn't much wanted to, unable to keep up with young Rodney's insatiable enthusiasm for shooting anything covered in feathers or fur—when he wasn't busy peeping through the maids' keyholes.

"*Tempus fugit*," Mrs. Smithings uttered wistfully, commenting on the all too swift passage of time.

"*Ita vero*," Rex agreed, already deploring his next birthday.

"Keeping up with your Latin, I see. I suppose you need it in your profession. Your mother tells me you took silk a few years ago. Do you still prosecute?"

"Aye, someone has to bring the criminals to justice. Just when I think I've heard what must surely be the last remaining mitigating plea ever to be dreamt up in someone's defense, I am surprised anew."

The last one, which he was too modest to cite in present company, being the PMS plea. A lawyer had actually argued that his client never would have doused her deceiving husband's *membrum virile* in lighter fluid and then set fire to it had she not been suffering from the hormonal effects of Aunt Flo's impending visit.

"Quite, but desperate times call for desperate measures," Dahlia Smithings remarked as though reading his thoughts. She crossed to the door. "I trust you will have a pleasant stay, in spite of this infernal snow."

"I'm sure I shall," Rex replied, bowing slightly as she left—at the same time wondering why he felt compelled to revert to such anachronistic behavior in her presence.

Closing the door, he began unbundling himself of surplus clothing. Mercifully, the puppy was still asleep in his pocket. Rex planted himself at the oak washstand that would have held a bowl and pitcher prior to indoor plumbing and now accommodated a sink. As he smoothed down his beard and whiskers, he speculated on the pair of single women from north-central England and the American lady whom Mrs. Smithings had mentioned.

He was not free *per se*—Mrs. Wilcox had fulfilled his bachelor needs quite satisfactorily since his wife passed away years before—and yet the company of women could add charm to a room. His mother's absence from Edinburgh would have provided an ideal opportunity to spend Christmas with Mrs. Wilcox, but alas, she too had left on an errand of mercy. His brush hung in midair as he pondered what might have befallen Moira. Even if the phone lines were down in her part of Baghdad, she could have written to him or at a pinch sent an e-mail if she had access to a computer. He wished he could have managed to persuade her to stay, but Moira Wilcox was a very stubborn woman.

The cold wind and exercise lent a ruddy glow to his already florid complexion, making the green of his eyes all the more vivid. Rex did not consider himself a vain man, but he believed in making the most of what God had seen fit to bestow upon him. Accordingly, he now donned the powder blue lamb's wool sweater his mother had knitted, fretting as she always did about his catching the flu, as if anywhere could be as bleak and bitter cold as Scotland in the depth of winter. With a glance at his watch, he decided to dispense with the unpacking and go down to tea. As he descended the stairs, he schemed how he might sneak some cake back up to his room for the stray puppy. He hoped it didn't bark. In his experience, the smaller the dog the more predisposed they were to yapping.

All seven of his fellow guests had congregated in the drawing room by the time he arrived. Mrs. Smithings adroitly made the introductions and then excused herself, leaving the others to sit with cups and saucers in hand, nibbling on cake and sizing up the newcomer.

"So you're an advocate from Edinburgh?" Anthony Smart asked from a fireside armchair, swinging his shoe over his knee. "Is that the same as a barrister?"

"Aye, it is."

"Do you defend the buggers or put them away?"

"Put them away. Almost without exception."

"Our dear Ms. Greenbaum is from New York, so I expect she is very familiar with your breed."

The lady in question, a forthright person of fifty or thereabouts, sat on a sofa jabbing at a handheld gadget. She peered at Rex over the rims of her glasses. "Hate them—can't live without them. Publishing lawyers aren't so bad. Criminal lawyers and personal injury attorneys are the worst."

"I'm a criminal lawyer."

"Ah, well. But then, it's a more respected profession in England."

"And Scotland."

Miriam Greenbaum looked blank as though she thought Scotland was in England, and Rex remembered why he sometimes lost patience with Americans.

"The poor man hasn't been here five minutes and here we are laying into him," the pretty blonde on the sofa said with a laugh.

Rex had already decided he preferred Helen d'Arcy of the three single female guests. She was approachably attractive, her thick, lackluster hair worn in a casual sweep to her shoulders, a pale shade of pink on her lips. Her friend Wanda looked the neurotic type, and the New Yorker came across as more irritating than a kilt with burrs up the inside. Yvette Perkins, the fourth female guest, sat Velcro-stuck to her husband on a loveseat located by one of the windows.

"Mrs. Smithings introduced you as Reginald, but you said you prefer to be called Rex for short?" the blonde inquired.

"Same Latin root. *Rex, regis,* meaning king. As long as you don't call me Reggie."

"My Latin's a bit rusty, I'm afraid. I haven't looked at it since school, and I'm not going to admit how long ago *that* is!"

"It canna be that long," Rex said gallantly, lifting his cup to his lips.

"I love your Scots accent." Wanda fluttered her spidery eyelashes at him. "You sound like a gruff Sean Connery, doesn't he, Helen?"

"We didn't study Latin at my school," Patrick Vance said, his looks marred by a gap between his front teeth as he smiled, gazing up from his sketchpad. He returned to his subject.

Following the direction of his line of vision, Rex saw a robin hop along the snowy ledge of the windowsill. Breathing in the wintry smell of burning logs and the lemony scent of furniture polish, he decided that Christmas would indeed have been lonely in Edinburgh. No doubt one of his legal colleagues would have invited him to Christmas dinner, but they would have probably ended up talking shop, and Rex wanted a break from case law and criminals…

"I left my smokes up in the room, luv," Charley told his wife. "D'you mind getting them while I have a word with the new guest?" Catching Rex's eye, he wandered to the window at the far end of the room and looked out at the snow that was taking on a bluish hue in the late afternoon.

"There'll be more snow tonight," the jolly-faced Cockney said as Rex approached.

"Aye, I was lucky to get here when I did. I was on the last train before they stopped the service, and even then we had to alight before we reached the station. There was packed ice blocking the tracks."

Charley nodded. "Me and Yvette are expected at her mum's for Christmas Eve. I don't know if that will happen now."

"Argh, I don't suppose newlyweds mind too much where they are as long as they're together in a nice warm bed."

"Right enough, and anyway I could give Christmas at Yvette's house a miss this year. Her mother's a bit of a busybody, well-meaning and all, but ..."

"So," Rex said, casually picking off a frayed end of wool from the sleeve of his blue sweater. "You wanted to talk to me."

"Yeah, that's the other reason I'm in no hurry to leave. I don't want to miss all the excitement—you know, when the police come and examine the body."

"The old man who had a stroke?"

"It wasn't a stroke, mate. He was poisoned, sure as I'm standing right here."

"Poisoned? How?"

"I'm certain his almond tart had cyanide in it. There was white foam at the corners of his mouth. That's what made me suspicious. What with the increased threat of terrorism and all, we have regular courses on poisons and what to do in the event of biochemical warfare. Dicobalt edetate in the case of cyanide and—"

"You are in the medical profession?"

"Paramedic."

"So you're saying he ate an almond tart and died as a result?"

"Looks that way. He only ate the filling. He couldn't manage the pastry with his dentures."

"Who else ate the tarts?"

"That's the funny thing," Charley said, scratching his ear. "I think everybody did, except maybe Anthony—you know, the ponce with the designer goatee? Well, he's a health nut from what I can make out, and I don't think he would have eaten one."

"And where is the rest of Mr. Lawdry's tart now?"

"I wrapped it in plastic and put it in my room for analysis in a lab when the police arrive."

"Did you tell anyone else about this?"

"Nah—didn't see the point in scaring people when no one can get to us. Imagine being cooped up in a house full of hysterical women."

"Quite. Well, I admire your *sang-froid.*"

"Sig Freud is my middle name," Charley joked, looking around the room. "Wonder where Yvette's got to? I'm dying for a fag."

"And you didn't call the police about it?"

"Like I said, what was the point? I decided to wait until they got here. Then when you arrived, I thought, Here's a man of the law—I can unburden my secret to him, sort of thing."

"I'd be glad to help, but I'd like to see your bit of evidence first, if I may."

They met Yvette on the stairs.

"Here you go," she said, handing Charley his cigarettes.

"Ta. Go on downstairs. I want to show Rex something."

The Perkins' suite was located in the east wing. Rex waited outside while Charley fetched the remains of the tart. Unwrapping it,

Rex sniffed and examined it. Most of the soft center between the fluted crust had been scooped out. He pulled a starched handkerchief from the pocket of his corduroys and dipped a corner into the filling. It tasted of sugary almonds, and something bitter and caustic besides.

"What d'you think?" Charley asked, eying him intently.

"The tart would have had to contain more than a sprinkling of cyanide to cause death, wouldn't it?"

"The heart is very susceptible to cyanide, and Lawdry had a weak heart. Everyone knew about it. He kept his pills on the dining room table. But you're right—it would have taken more than a sprinkling. It's a bit of a coincidence, what with cyanide tasting like almonds and all ..."

"The filling does have a slightly peculiar taste. All the same, it would help if we could establish the presence of cyanide in the house."

"The culprit like as not got rid of the evidence. We'd have to search the house from attic to cellar. Fat chance we'd find anything, or even know what we were looking for. Perhaps you should take a look at the body."

"Aye, though I'm no medical examiner. You'd know more about the effects of poisoning than I, so I'm just going to have to take your word for it until we can get a drug screen report."

"A heart attack wouldn't have caused frothing at the mouth," Charley insisted.

Rex made a mental note to sound out the other guests about how Lawdry looked at the time of death. "It is a wee bit suspicious," he agreed. "Perhaps I should ask Mrs. Smithings about the staff."

"I wish you would because I've been a bit off my food, wondering if arsenic's going to turn up in the soup. Know what I mean?"

The same thought was beginning to occur to Rex, and he had been so looking forward to a proper Christmas dinner with all the trimmings.

There was no time to lose. If Charley was right, they had to find out why and how the old man ended up with a poisoned iced tart.

THREE

Leaving Charley at the honeymoon suite, Rex went back down to the foyer and knocked at the parlor-office door. Without waiting for a response, he entered a room formally and abundantly furnished in the Victorian tradition—upholstered sofas in burgundy velvet and ornate mahogany tables, every available surface crammed with Oriental vases, statuettes, and framed photographs.

Over the mantelpiece hung a curved Gurkha knife with a stitched leather scabbard that Rex remembered from childhood. The thin form of Mrs. Smithings bent over a ball-and-claw footed writing desk, an Edwardian cradle phone within her reach. With an expression of vague annoyance, she looked up at him from above a pair of reading spectacles perched on her aquiline nose.

"I hope I'm not disturbing you," he apologized. "I came to discuss the matter of your deceased guest."

Mrs. Smithings sat upright. "Well, you had better shut the door and sit down."

Rex did so. "The long and the short of it is that Charley Perkins, who is a paramedic, thought he noticed some irregularities concerning Henry Lawdry's death."

"I see."

"He appears convinced the old man was poisoned by a dose of cyanide that somehow found its way into his almond tart."

"Preposterous."

"So it would seem, but I thought it prudent to advise you, in the remote event it might be true. Now, is there any member of your staff capable of committing such an act?"

"The very idea!"

"Mrs. Smithings, I know how hard it must be for you to even consider such a thing, but I must warn you: Charley Perkins intends going to the police with this. If there are grounds for his allegations, it would not look well if we were seen to be remiss in taking the appropriate action."

Rex knew he sounded pompous, but Mrs. Smithings had that effect on him. A fax machine stashed in her desk whirred and beeped incongruously.

"What do you propose we do?" she asked.

"I'd like to interview the staff—discreetly, of course. And I suggest that no more tarts be made available for consumption."

"There are no more," Mrs. Smithings replied archly.

"When were they baked?"

"Yesterday after lunch. Please proceed with caution, Reginald. Any suspicion of a scandal would bode ill for my business."

"I quite understand. Can you tell me who was in the kitchen yesterday?"

"The cook, naturally. Sandy Bellows has been with me for six years. Louise comes in from the village to clean, but was unable to yesterday and today due to the snow. Mrs. Bellows, who starts early to prepare breakfast, arrived yesterday before the worst of the weather. Rosie Porter is in and out of the kitchen. Her duties mainly entail waiting upon the guests. She lives in."

Rex was well aware of Rosie, who'd brought in the tea earlier. Hard *not* to notice the sloe-eyed, dark-haired beauty with cheeks red as apples. She was the sort of girl who brought to mind such bawdy expressions as "comely wench" and "tumbling in the hay"— and visions of bosomy rollicking behind the hawthorn hedge of a May evening...

"And then there is that useless creature Clifford Beadel, whom you saw when you arrived," Mrs. Smithings was saying. "Perhaps you remember him from all those years ago."

"And what does he do?"

"Clifford just creaks along doing odd jobs in the house and garden. He lives alone in the lodge by the gate."

"You said yesterday that his family has always been at Swanmere Manor. What about Rosie?"

"Rosie Porter has been with me for eighteen months. She is a most loyal and able employee."

"Thank you, Mrs. Smithings. I won't take up any more of your time at present."

"Are you going to talk to the staff about cyanide and ruin everyone's Christmas?" If looks could freeze, Rex would have turned into a snowman.

"I don't think I need bring that up. My questions will be of a general nature. I'll explain that I'm an old friend of the family.

From what you've told me, none of the three servants seem to be of the murdering persuasion. I just want to see what, if anything, comes up."

"Very well. And what about the guests?"

"Not at this point. Charley and I have agreed to keep the matter to ourselves and just observe."

"Good. It's trying enough for the guests not to be able to leave the hotel."

"I would like to see Mr. Lawdry's room, however."

"Really? How gruesome." Dahlia Smithings fingered her pearl choker. "We put plastic beneath him and covered him up with a sheet. I have no idea what state he will be in now. Well, take this master key. It's the one I give Louise to make up the rooms. And one more thing, Reginald ... Did your mother knit you that sweater?"

"Aye, she did."

"I thought so. She always did lack taste in clothes. The blue clashes most dreadfully with your red hair. I just thought I should mention it."

"Er, thank you." Feeling like he'd just been brought to task by a school headmistress for not wiping his nose, Rex got up and, careful not to upset the numerous delicate items that impeded his bulky progress to the door, gratefully left Mrs. Smithings' presence.

Charley was hovering outside the door. "How did it go?" he asked in a hushed voice.

"I can talk to the staff, but Mrs. Smithings thinks I'm on a wild goose chase."

"Maybe it was the old bat herself who did Henry in."

"Why would she want to murder a paying guest?"

Charley shrugged. "Why would *anyone* want to murder him?"

"I canna imagine. But there must be a connection somewhere." Rex checked his watch. "There's someone in London I need to call. He clerks for a friend of mine. Perhaps he can look into Lawdry's background and come up with a motive for someone to kill him. First you need to tell me everything you know about the old man."

"Yvette could tell you more. She spent quite a bit of time with Henry, said she felt sorry for him. Yvette's soft-hearted that way. She was playing Tiddlywinks with him just before tea yesterday."

"I'll talk to her. Oh, by the way, Charley, is there anything wrong with my sweater?"

"Is it back to front?"

"No, I don't think so."

"Oh, I get it. It's inside out."

"The colour, man. Is it a bit loud?"

"Oh! Nah, I wouldn't say that. But then I'm a bit colour blind myself. You'd have to ask Yvette. Yvette, luv," he called into the drawing room where she sat chatting to Helen, and knitting a scarf. "Rex wants a word. In private."

"I'll be in the library," Rex told him, crossing the foyer.

He put a quick call through to the office of Browne, Quiggley & Squire, thankful that the law clerk was working late and that the library was deserted so he could conduct his conversation in private. The lamp on the leather-top partners' desk formed a pool of light, leaving the outer reaches of the room in darkness. As Rex waited for Yvette, he contemplated, within the illuminated radius, an antique still life of flowers and pears mellowed with age and encased by books—though in his mind's eye he was seeing the remains of Lawdry's pastry.

Poison, Rex mused, was often a woman's recourse, or a doctor's. Charley had pharmaceutical knowledge and could not be ruled out, even if he had been the one to alert Rex to the possibility of cyanide in the first place—perhaps as a bluff?

Presently, Yvette joined him and, after assuring him that his sweater was nice, very nice indeed, and much better purl work than she could ever do herself, proceeded to tell him what she knew about Henry Lawdry. In her jeans and fleecy cardigan, Rex thought she looked barely old enough to be married. "Why are you asking about him?" she asked.

"I thought I'd write a wee obituary."

"Oh, how sweet of you. From what he told me, he doesn't have any family except that estranged son in Melbourne. He said he had no one to leave his money to. His son has done very well for himself in Australia. I don't expect he'll find out about his father's death until he's contacted by the solicitor. Don't forget to mention Henry was one of the first paratroopers to land in Normandy in World War II," Yvette added proudly.

Rex thanked her and, thumbing the master key in his pocket, went upstairs. Just as he set foot on the landing, he heard a squeak and saw the brass doorknob turn in number four. What was somebody doing in the dead man's room? Flattening himself against the wall, he held his breath. The door clicked shut and steps approached down the carpet. Light on his feet for a man of his proportions, Rex darted back into the stairwell in time to glimpse a petite brunette pass along the landing toward the east wing. Close call, he thought, wondering what business Wanda Martyr had in that room.

Once the coast was clear, he inserted his key into the lock and eased open the door. The room felt colder than a tomb in spite of his warm sweater and woolen gloves. The drapes drawn across the open window admitted a ghostly light. An unusual smell, beyond what he'd expected, made him think of church. He shivered.

The deceased was laid out on a handsome sleigh bed, a sheet draped over his body. Rex switched on the bedside lamp and turned back the sheet, exposing an old face touched with the dignity and pallor of death. He noticed the empty left sleeve. Slipping his fingers into the jacket pockets, Rex encountered small smooth discs and pulled out a couple of Tiddlywinks. After re-covering the body, he inspected the items on the dressing table, which included a starched handkerchief monogrammed "H.D.L."

Back on the landing, he let out a shuddering sigh. Since viewing his father in a coffin at age seven, Rex felt shaken to the core whenever confronted by mortality. Death had not made sense to him then, and the words spoken by the minister at the graveside, "The Lord giveth and the Lord taketh away," failed to comfort him to this day.

Clutching the banister, he made his way down to the drawing room where Patrick Vance sat by the fireside smoking a cigarette. Rex decided to take advantage of finding the young man alone to sound him out about Lawdry. Artists typically had a keen eye. "Not sketching?" he asked.

"I'm pretty much running out of subject matter. I may add some colour to the robin later."

"I admire your talent. I don't have a creative bone in my body."

"Still, you know Latin," Patrick retorted with a grin, revealing the gap in his teeth which lent him a demonic air.

Rex picked up the matchbox balancing on the armrest. The lid depicted Swanmere Manor, a surprising concession to commercialism on Mrs. Smithings' part. "I heard there was a death in this room yesterday," he prompted. "Not what you were all expecting, I'm sure."

"Hardly. One minute the old man is chatting away about his dentures, the next—dead as a doorpost!" Patrick described the scene at tea.

After interjecting a few questions, Rex felt he had a good idea of who was where and who did and said what. "Where's Anthony?" he asked.

"Napping. He'd kill me if he found me smoking. Miriam can't abide it either, so she's working on her precious manuscript in the library at the far side of the house. Don't get me wrong, not all Yanks are bad. Some of our American clients at Smart Design are very cultured and have impeccable taste. Most are from New York. Miriam just rubs me up the wrong way."

"Aye, I know what you mean. How do you get on with Wanda?"

"Wanda?" Patrick blew out a puff of smoke in a disdainful manner. "She'd be all right if she stopped harping on about her bloody divorce. Why d'you ask?"

"A curious thing, really. I could swear I saw her come out of Lawdry's room just now. I wonder who gave her the key…"

"I wouldn't go in there if you paid me."

"Perhaps she had a special affection for the old man."

With an immaculately kept hand, Patrick stubbed out his cigarette in the bronze ashtray. "I don't think so, not really. Helen spent more time with him, and so did Yvette. Old Lawdry was quite the ladies' man! Ah, well, may God rest his soul and all that."

"Amen. Anyhow, I'll leave you to your solitude, see what's brewing in the kitchen." Hands in his pockets, Rex sauntered down the hall to the spacious scrubbed kitchen where a robust older woman in an apron was sautéing diced celery, carrots, onions, and chili pepper in an industrial-size wok. "Mm, is that curry I smell?" he asked.

"It is," the woman said, pouring in stock and adding lentils and shredded chicken. She wore her hair close-cropped and sported multiple piercings in her left ear. "I'm making Mulligatawny Soup for tonight. Mrs. Smithings brought the recipe back from India in 1949 when her husband was serving over there."

"I think I may have had it one time when I stayed here as a lad. You must be Sandy Bellows, the cook. Mrs. Smithings has been singing your praises to my mother."

"Has she now?" The cook's face flushed with pleasure.

Rex introduced himself and assumed a casual pose leaning against the counter. "Mrs. Smithings said you've been working here six years."

"Sounds about right." While she chopped apples, Sandy Bellows chatted on about how fortunate it was she'd prepared much of the food in advance with Louise's help—before the snow terminated all access and egress from the hotel.

"I understand the almond tarts went down a treat. It's a pity I wasn't here yesterday to try one."

"The almond tarts are my own recipe. I like nut desserts at Christmas as they're so festive." The cook threw handfuls of basmati rice into a saucepan. "I don't see how that poor old man could have choked on one of them tarts, like they first said. More likely it was a heart attack. And I was just saying to Mrs. Smithings yesterday what a shame it was, him being alone this time of year."

"Do any of the guests ever come into the kitchen?"

The cook proceeded to mince parsley. "Not usually, though that Mr. Smart did come in yesterday before tea. He wanted to know if we used organic products in the cooking. Said he was into health. And then that American woman is in and out, very fond of food she is, but has to watch her weight."

"Don't we all." Rex patted his belly.

"Oh, come now. You're a fine figure of a man."

"Why, thank you for that, Mrs. Bellows. Still, it's a lot of work for you, cooking for all these people ..."

"We *have* been short-handed the last two days. Rosie's run off her feet but she helps when she can, and Clifford ... Well, I have to watch what I say as he's probably earwigging in the scullery. He's not as deaf as he makes out. Oh, he's a cunning one, is that old bodger." She wiped her hands on her apron. "Well, that's everything simmering nicely. I think I'll go upstairs and put my feet up before I have to see to the main course."

When she left, Rex poked his head around the scullery door and found Clifford seated at an old wooden table, polishing a pair of silver candlesticks. The metallic tang of Brasso filled the whitewashed room, all but smothering the reek of mildew rising from the assortment of Wellington boots, mackintoshes, and umbrellas stacked by the door beside a pile of flowerpots and gardening utensils.

"Just came for a smoke," Rex said, pulling his pipe from his pocket. "You don't mind, do you? It's too cold to stand outside."

"Ar, de cold be purty bad. Eh don' mind de bacca if ye don' mind de slummocky table 'ere."

Without fully understanding what the old man had said, Rex took this as an invitation to fill his pipe. The fragrant aroma of Clan tobacco helped snuff out the Brasso and mildew. Propping up the door frame while sucking on his pipe stem, Rex pondered how to tackle him. "Problem with rodents?" he asked, pointing to the box of rat poison on one of the shelves.

"Ar. She won't have cats 'round the place. Dogs neither."

Rex assumed Clifford was referring to Mrs. Smithings. "That's a pity because I smuggled a stray puppy into my room. You won't tell Mrs. Smithings, will you?"

Clifford grinned slyly and shook his head.

"So, you're entrusted with the family silver?" Rex asked.

"Ar."

"There must be a lot of heirlooms in the home."

"Ar. But she 'ad to sell a lot to pay off the master's debts." Clifford seemed to relish imparting this little tidbit of gossip—his ferrety eyes gleamed. "Not the jewellery though. Still plenty of that to clean."

"You take care of that too?"

"Nar. Not since me 'ands got the screws. The work's too fiddly for a body wi' rheumatics."

"Who cleans it then?"

"The Porter girl did it last."

"Rosie."

"Nar, her sister wot worked here before."

At that moment, Rex heard a rap at the window and saw Charley gesticulating frantically at him to come outside. Rex opened the scullery door.

"You'll never guess what I found in the rubbish," the young Cockney hissed. "There was tons to sift through since it's not been collected for days because of the snow. Look." He pulled a container from its newspaper wrapping. "Sodium Cyanide—it says right here on the label."

FOUR

Now that the existence of cyanide had been established, Rex felt it his duty to Mrs. Smithings to get to the bottom of Lawdry's death. As her oldest friend, his mother would expect it of him. He expected it of himself. He could not imagine getting back on the train to Edinburgh with the case unresolved.

Filching a few scraps of chicken from the kitchen counter, Rex wrapped them in his handkerchief and made his way back to the foyer. As he passed the parlor-office, he heard Mrs. Smithings' shrill voice behind the door: "Tears won't do, do you hear? We must keep a stiff upper lip. There's nothing to be done about it now."

"Yes, ma'am. I'll try harder, ma'am."

"See that you do. Now run along, Rosie, and attend to your duties."

The next moment, the door flew open and the girl almost collided with Rex as he loitered by the stairs, emptying his pipe bowl into an ashtray. She wiped her eyes on her apron and gave him a defiant little smile.

"Is everything okay, lass?" he asked kindly.

"I'm still a bit upset about Mr. Lawdry. It's a shame, really. He was a likeable old man. Always very polite and grateful when I brought him anything. Not like that Wanda Martyr. I think she enjoys treating me like a servant. It's, 'Rosie, can you do this?', 'Oh, Rosie, would you do that?' Lazy cow."

Rex ducked his chin into his other chin, suppressing a smile. "Have you been working here long?" he asked.

"Since last summer. Mrs. Smithings is a really good employer, gives me a weekend off every month to visit my family in London."

"Oh, I took you for a fresh-faced Sussex girl."

"The country air does wonders for a girl's complexion," Rosie said with a strained laugh. "But London born and bred, I am."

"Quite a change, then. What do you do here?"

"At work? I waitress. The cleaning staff come in mornings but not since the blizzard, so I help with making up the beds and such as well."

"Do you ever help out in the kitchen?"

"Only when we're shorthanded."

"Like now, I imagine."

"Yes, but Mrs. Bellows prepared a lot in advance, stuffed the freezer sort of thing. The pastries are fresh-baked every day, of course."

"Did you help with the almond tarts?"

Rosie gave a start of surprise. "No, they were ready on a tray for me to take in. Are you asking these questions because of Mr. Lawdry's death? It was to be expected—he was in poor health."

"So I understand, but Mrs. Smithings agreed that I should talk to the staff." Rosie's plum-dark eyes slid to her employer's door. "So—you served tea in the drawing room," Rex continued. "Did everyone partake of the almond tarts?"

"Well, the newlyweds weren't down yet. All the other guests were there. Then I left. Mr. Smart doesn't eat sweets. The two women friends—the Abs-Fabs Duo I call them—they always make a big to-do about watching their weight, but they eat whatever's put in front of them. The American is the same way."

"Where did you put the tray?"

"On the round table. I let everyone help themselves. They all know tea is at four thirty, but not everyone's here on the dot, so I just leave them to it."

"Just one more question, Rosie. Do you recall who was in the kitchen when you picked up the tray?"

"Cook and Mrs. Smithings. And when I got back, Clifford was there mucking in with the potatoes."

After he left Rosie, Rex bounded up the stairs, reflecting that there never would have been any suspicion of cyanide poisoning, had Charlie not been around to attend to Lawdry. And he himself would not be in the process of questioning the staff and taking more than a casual interest in the guests. So much for his relaxing Christmas.

He fed the puppy the chicken scraps and decided to join his fellow guests in the drawing room for further observation. There might be more to them than met the eye, and it was just conceivable one of them had managed to slip the cyanide directly into Lawdry's tart. As he stepped out of his room, Mrs. Dahlia Smithings was coming up the stairs.

"Did you find out anything of interest?" she asked.

"Well," Rex said, drawing closer to her. "Charley found an empty container of sodium cyanide in the dustbin outside."

"Ah, yes. Well, we use that for cleaning jewellery and such. We buy it by the pound from a pharmaceutical company in Brighton."

Rex coughed politely. "A fact you omitted to mention earlier on, Mrs. Smithings."

"It slipped my mind. Things do at my age, you know."

He showed her the container. "Is this the jar?"

"I believe so."

"Where did you keep it?"

"On a shelf in the scullery with the other cleaning products."

"Clifford said the jewellery hasna been cleaned in awhile."

"Clifford! I'm surprised you were able to make out his gibberish. He speaks that way on purpose, you know."

"This does rather support Charley's theory of poisoning, deliberate or otherwise …"

"Charley may be making it all up and have planted the container himself."

"Aye, but the lad is a medic and he seems to have his head screwed on tight. I canna see him doing this just to create a bit o' drama."

"Young men are prone to pulling pranks."

Ah, yes—Rodney. Her son had certainly been one for pranks. Mrs. Smithings looked wistful, as though she were thinking of him at that moment.

"Rodney died a hero," he said. "You must be proud of him."

Her lips tightened into a thin line. "Since my son is not here, what can he possibly have to do with any of this?"

"I'm sorry," Rex stammered, somewhat perplexed. Most mothers wanted to talk about their sons, living or dead. His own mother bored the ears off the ladies of the Morningside—genteelly pronounced *Moarningsaide*—tea and scone set with accounts of his professional exploits. When she received visitors, she had him buy flowers—*Nothing extravagant, mind*—so she could boast that her doting son had given them to her.

He was on the point of asking Mrs. Smithings about Rosie's sister when his cell phone trilled in his pocket. The LCD listed a London number. He excused himself and hurried back to his room to take the call in private. "Thaddeus," he said. "Any luck?"

The young law clerk at the other end informed him that he'd managed to get hold of Lawdry's solicitor and that the old man had not died intestate after all, having left everything to Claws, his cat. No human had stood to gain by his death, and Thaddeus could find no ties between the deceased and any of the hotel staff or guests, whose names and addresses Rex had supplied him from the guest book in the hall.

"I did find out that Anthony Smart was up on a charge of drunk and disorderly behaviour at a gay bar last year, but got off with a fine," the clerk said. "Is there anything else you'd like me to check out?"

Rex said he would be in touch—right now he was at a dead end. Henry Lawdry's alleged murder was without apparent motive.

———

Rex noticed the puppy sniffing items around the walls of his room and getting ready to raise its hind leg against a giant potted fern.

"Argh, noo," he said, scooping him up in his arms. "Ye canna do that."

He took the dog downstairs and through the scullery to the back door, leaving him in Clifford's care. "Och, I'll be back later," Rex said when it looked up at him in reproach through the raccoon markings around its eyes.

He ambled into the drawing room where most of the guests were biding time until dinner, and took up a position by one of the west-facing windows. The white-blanketed lawns disappeared into darkness.

"I love doing hair," Patrick Vance was saying, "and Anthony has so little. If you have the rollers, I have the time."

Turning around, Rex saw that the young man was addressing Wanda Martyr. Helen nodded to her friend in encouragement.

"When do you want to do it?" Wanda asked Patrick.

"How about after dinner?"

"All right then. That way I'll look fab for Christmas Eve. After all, it's not like there's a whole lot to do around here."

"I feel like I'm living in a Christmas card, the time we spend in this room," Helen agreed. "It's all very pretty, of course, but I'm beginning to get cabin fever."

"Aye," Rex said from the window. "And I came down from Scotland thinking I might play a bit o' tennis and do some hiking." He sought an armchair among the guests. Only the honeymooners were absent.

"Wanda and I managed to get some walking in before the snow started," Helen told him. "We took the bridle path between Eastbourne and Alfriston, and crossed the downs above the ancient Long Man. It's the size of a football field and cut out of the chalk.

And there's a pretty Norman church in Jevington that's worth a visit too."

As Rex observed once again, Helen was an attractive woman with a cheerful and sensible air about her. "I came here as a boy," he told her. "It was summer—buttercups and red campion everywhere. There was a place we used to call Bluebell Valley. I was fond of nature rambles and badger-watching back then. Aye, I would've liked to have done some walking meself."

"This hotel needs more activities," Patrick said. "For a start, the old conservatory is never used. I'd put in a huge jacuzzi, paint a tropical fresco, and install lots of exotic plants."

"We could convert the library into a pool room," Anthony suggested.

Helen smiled. "I doubt Mrs. Smithings would approve of your renovations."

"Mrs. Mothballs needs to move with the times. She should retire and have someone manage the place for her."

Beyond the French doors, a ring-tone blared out the Star Spangled Banner. "I made it to page 30 of the manuscript you sent up," Miriam Greenbaum told her caller, "and I have to say I just didn't get off on it. The writing was nowhere near ready for prime time ... Uh-huh. Uh-huh. Send the standard rejection."

With the arrival of Ms. Greenbaum, Rex observed an atmosphere of constraint settle upon the guests. Wanda, in particular, made no effort to veil her hostility, staring pointedly at the intruder. She was a woman who wore her emotions on display. Helen, on the other hand, with a barely perceptible tightening of the jaw, confined herself to studying a women's magazine with probably more attention than it deserved. Patrick and Anthony, exchanging a glance of complicity as Miriam crossed to a vacant sofa, took up their books in unison.

She appeared not to notice the sudden cessation of chatter. Pushing her glasses up her nose, she pulled a manuscript from a box file and became engrossed in its contents, from time to time scratching annotations in the margin with a blue pen.

"Does anyone know where the name Swanmere comes from?" Rex asked his neighbors, after a few minutes of awkward silence.

"*Mere* means 'pond', doesn't it?" Wanda said, stretching her elegantly slippered feet toward the fire. "There's a big pond down by the village. It's frozen up now, but there are swans there."

"I'd like to sketch it," Patrick said wistfully. "Swans are such graceful creatures."

"Oh, you have to be careful," Helen interjected. "The cob has a wingspan of eight feet. They can be quite vicious, you know, coming at you with flapping wings and outstretched beaks …"

Finally, Rosie summoned the guests to dinner.

In the dining room, the wainscoting below the flocked wallpaper was just as Rex remembered it. The Victorian dresser displaying a Royal Albert service still stood in a corner. It was as though time had stood still. Heavy brocade curtains shut out the frigid night, while a crystal chandelier cast its glow upon the guests seated at the table spread with white linen. Rex was pleased to find that his place, reserved by a hand-written name card, was beside Helen.

"How's the wee dog doing?" he asked Clifford, who crouched by the hearth, banking up the fire.

"I 'ad to put 'im in the cellar."

"What dog is this?" Miriam Greenbaum demanded from across the table.

"A stray I found shivering in the snow on my way to the hotel this afternoon."

"Oh, bless you," Helen said. "Why can't we have him in here with us?"

"A dog would make it seem more homey," Wanda Martyr added, unfolding her napkin.

"Aye, but from what I hear Mrs. Smithings won't have it in the house. No doubt she sees it as a health hazard."

"I should think the almond tarts are more of a hazard," Anthony quipped, presiding at the head of the table.

"Mrs. Smithings should have turned this place into a boarding school," Ms. Greenbaum remarked. "There are more rules and regulations at Swanmere Manor than in a sorority house."

Rex chuckled. "Aye, she's already made me feel like an ill-favoured schoolboy on occasion."

"What sort of dog is it?" Helen asked.

"A Jack Russell terrier, I believe. He's a bonny wee thing."

Miriam Greenbaum grabbed a bread roll. "Well, the old harridan can't very well turn him out into the snow. And the cellar's no better. It must be icy cold down there."

The guests heatedly debated what to do about the dog while Rosie filled the water glasses.

"So what's on the menu tonight, Rosie," Anthony inquired. "I brought up red and white wine from the cellar."

"Oh, you should have sent Clifford down for it," Rosie said.

"The cellar steps are steep and badly lit. It's too dangerous for an old fellow like Clifford." Anthony looked around for him, but he had already left the room.

Sandy Bellows, beaming in a starched white apron, brought in a silver tureen wafting wreaths of steam, and set it down on the table. The soup's surface was swirled with cream and sprinkled with fresh parsley. The guests immediately launched into a volley of speculations as to what sort of soup it might be.

"Smells deliciously like curry," Patrick said.

The cook began ladling it into bowls. "It's Mulligatawny, which means 'pepper water' in Indian. Just the ticket for a cold winter's night."

"This claret is corked," Anthony announced testily. "I'll have to run down to the cellar and get another bottle."

"Anthony is our self-appointed sommelier," Patrick explained to Rex as his partner left the room. "Mrs. Smithings is teetotal and knows nothing about wine. When Anthony discovered yesterday that the late Colonel kept a respectable cellar, he suggested we drink some of it before it goes bad. Mrs. Smithings is only charging twelve pounds a bottle."

"Thank goodness for Anthony," Miriam Greenbaum chimed in. "I don't know about the rest of you but I'm ready for some booze. The sherry didn't even begin to tickle the spot."

Wanda and Helen concurred wholeheartedly. Mrs. Bellows removed the tureen from the table and entreated the guests to enjoy their soup.

"I'll go with Anthony and rescue that poor dog," Miriam declared, getting up from her chair.

"Oh, yes, do," Helen said. "Shall I come with you?"

"No, I'll manage. Go ahead and start without us."

Recalling the cyanide in the tart, Rex tentatively dipped his spoon in his soup and eyed Patrick, Wanda, and Helen to see if they were hesitant to taste theirs. They all attacked the Mulligatawny with gusto, but before Helen could put her spoon to her lips, her cell phone rang.

"Blast," she said, extracting it from her cardigan pocket and checking the display. "Oh, it's Pauline. Excuse me while I take this call," she told her dinner companions as she rose from the table. "Pauline? How are you, dear?" Her voice trailed off as she left the room.

"That's one of her special cases at the school where she counsels," Wanda explained. "Pauline is from a broken home and has serious substance-abuse problems. But she's a promising student and Helen has taken her under her wing."

"Helen seems like a very nice person," Patrick commented, mopping up the soup with his bread.

"Yes, she is. And she has really helped me through my divorce. She's a wonderful listener. I can't imagine this is much of a holiday for her."

Rex risked some of the soup himself. "Aye, 'tis spicy, right enough." Feeling his lips start a slow burn, he reached for his water glass.

"Fantastic for clearing the sinuses," Patrick said, taking a hanky from his pocket and blowing his nose. "I must get the recipe from old Bellows. Well, hello, you lovebirds. Deigning to join us at last?"

The honeymooners sheepishly took their places across from Rex. "Where are the others?" Charley asked.

"Anthony went to fetch some wine, Miriam left to rescue Rex's dog, and Helen had to take an important call," Patrick summarized.

"You have a dog?" Yvette asked Rex.

Before Rex could answer, Anthony burst into the dining room. "Oh, God! Oh, God! Miriam had a bad fall. I think she broke her neck!" he cried.

The table jostled with a rattle of china as the guests rose in haste. Rex bade Charley go with him and everyone else stay. Helen stepped into the dining room just as Rex and Charley were leaving. "What's wrong?" she asked.

"It's the American woman..." Charley blurted, rushing past her.

Rex heard Helen's gasp but did not stop. Anthony followed the two men into the deserted kitchen. On the pine table, Rex noticed the soup tureen and the pair of candlesticks that Clifford had been polishing in the scullery that afternoon.

"Careful," Anthony said when Rex approached the cellar. "There's ice melting on the steps. Looks like she might have slipped on it."

Rex sidestepped the ice and gingerly made his way to the bottom with one hand on the wall, Charley behind him carrying a lit candlestick. Miriam Greenbaum's body lay face first at the bottom of the stone steps, her neck twisted to the side, the thick-rimmed glasses askew beside her.

Charley placed the candlestick on the flagstone floor and felt for a pulse. "She's a gonner," he murmured. "Just like poor old Lawdry. And look here. She couldn't have got this contusion on the back of her neck from falling headlong."

Rex studied the red welt. "We'll have to leave the body here exactly as we found it." He looked around the musty cellar, bare except for broken garden furniture, a stack of chopped wood, and racks of wine. Finding a rock that had crumbled from the chalkstone wall, he outlined the deceased's body as a precaution. He wanted it left unmoved until the authorities arrived.

Anthony was waiting, ashen-faced, at the door to the cellar.

"Where were you when she fell?" Rex asked him as he reached the top of the steps.

"I was looking through the wine down there, checking the labels for another bottle of claret. My back was turned."

"It's dark in the cellar. How could you see what you were doing?"

"I had the candlestick with me. The one Charley's holding. Suddenly I heard a startled scream and turned around just in time to see Miriam land at the bottom of the steps. When I got to her, her eyes were—just staring."

"Did you touch her?"

"I turned her chin toward me so I could see her face. I wish I'd been nicer to her. She wasn't such a bad sort, really."

Rex looked around as he closed the cellar door. "Where's the dog?"

"Never saw him."

"Was anyone in the kitchen?"

"No, but I passed Mrs. Bellows in the corridor."

Rex turned to Charley. "Put that candlestick on the table and don't let anyone touch it, or the other one for that matter. And keep an eye on the staff when they reappear. Where *is* everybody?"

He crossed the kitchen to the scullery where he found the puppy curled up on a blanket on the floor, fast asleep. The rest of the room crouched in darkness. Flicking on the light switch, he found Clifford cowering by the umbrellas, a terrified look in his beady eyes.

"Ar, 'twas me," the old man mumbled, backing into the raincoats. "Don' tell her. She'll turn me out o' the lodge."

"What are you hiding?" Rex asked, grabbing the man's shoulder and spinning him around.

The old man clutched an empty decanter of sherry. "Don' tell her! An' I won' tell 'bout yer dog!"

The scent of sherry on Clifford's breath made Rex take a step back. "How long have you been in here?"

"Eh took the wood down the cellar. Then eh seed the sherry an' thought 'ow even she couldn't grudge me some at Christmastime and me 'ands so painful from the cold."

"Who was in the kitchen?"

"Don' rightly remember." Clifford's eyes took on a glassy sheen.

Rex held him steady. "Try."

"Her was there, an' Rosie an' Cook, thas right, cos they was all complainin' about me trackin' ice in on me boots. Only Cook was around when eh come back. She was at the stove wi' her back turned so eh wus able to sneak the dog an' the sherry past her."

"Did you hear anything afterwards?"

"I 'eard voices."

"A man's voice, woman's voice …?"

"An American voice."

"How did she sound?"

"Cross."

"What else?"

"Eh be deaf an' the wind be rattlin' the panes and that, so eh didn't hear much else, 'cept fer a thud." Clifford considered a moment, screwing up his eyes with the effort of concentration. "A dull sound like a rollin' pin hittin' pastry. Be ye gwene to tell her?"

"Tell Mrs. Smithings about the sherry? No, but keep an eye on the dog."

When Rex re-entered the kitchen, the other members of the staff were assembled around the table with Charley. Upon questioning them as to whether anybody had touched the candlesticks since Clifford polished them and receiving three answers in the negative, Rex sighed heavily, and said, "So we have another death in the house."

Rosie gazed at him wide-eyed. "I was in the drawing room collecting the cups and saucers and when I got back here, the American guest had fallen down the cellar steps!"

"And, Mrs. Bellows, where were you when all this was going on?"

"Powdering my nose down the hall."

"And I was upstairs," Dahlia Smithings exclaimed. "Those steps are dangerous. I warned Mr. Smart, but he fancies himself as a wine connoisseur and will go rummaging in the cellar. At least he is fit and agile. The Greenbaum woman should have had more sense. I heard she was going after a dog! Now we have another mishap on our hands."

"I think it was more than a mishap," Rex said, fishing Ms. Green-baum's goopy BlackBerry out of the soup tureen. "Why on earth would she have dropped this in the Mulligatawny? No, two deaths in two days are too much of a coincidence for me."

FIVE

Two deaths in a row. What on earth was going on, Rex wondered, and why the devil did they have to coincide with his trip? Deploring his luck, he made a detour into the drawing room to see if he could find a contact in New York to whom he might convey news of Ms. Greenbaum's death. He remembered seeing an address label for the literary agency on the title page of the manuscript she was working on. However, the box file on the sofa turned out to be empty, except for a blue pen and a key for room number eight.

Slipping upstairs, he found neither the manuscript nor a hard-copy address book in her room. Any data stored on her BlackBerry would have been destroyed when it fell in the soup. The biography of President Bush had to be somewhere. Had Miriam Greenbaum even come upstairs before dinner? Rex had been discussing swans with the other guests . . . No, he was sure she had not left the drawing room before Rosie summoned them into dinner. So where was the manuscript?

By the time he returned to the dining room, the soup plates had been cleared, and a stunned silence prevailed. The manuscript was not here either, and in any case, he didn't recall Miriam bringing it in to dinner.

"What's the verdict, Counsel?" Patrick asked. "Accident or foul play?"

"It appears Ms. Greenbaum received a blow to the neck, as you've no doubt all heard by now, and suspiciously enough, her e-mailing device was all but submerged in the soup tureen in the kitchen."

"Whatever was it doing in there?" Yvette asked.

"Good question. Unless someone didn't want it going off and giving away her location in the cellar."

"But we all knew she was going down there," Wanda pointed out.

"Aye, we at table knew."

"Getting rid of the BlackBerry might have been a wasted precaution," Helen said. "I lost my call and couldn't get a signal anywhere in the house."

"Did you by any chance go into the kitchen?"

"I wandered down that way but I didn't actually go in."

"Did you see anyone?"

"I can't recall. I was desperately trying to get Pauline back. She would only phone in an emergency, otherwise she'd leave a text message. She has an abusive stepdad. Oh, I hope nothing happened to her." Helen twisted her napkin compulsively. "I went to the foyer to use the hotel phone, but the line must be down with all the snow. Then I went to tell Mrs. Smithings, but she wasn't in her office or in the drawing room."

Rex drew a quick map in his head. The only way to the kitchen was along the hall past the drawing room and dining room, unless you went outside and around the house to the scullery door, which would be almost impossible with all the fresh snow. Still, he decided to check. "Hang on," he said, rising from his chair. "I'll be right back."

He hurried across the foyer to the front door. Upon opening it, a blast of chill air hit his face. The snow beyond the steps lay undisturbed—no one had used that door. Down the driveway, as though through a snow globe, he could just make out the tiny red brick gatehouse with its built-out bay window and flint-walled garden.

Pondering events, he closed the door. If everyone were to be believed, no one saw Miriam enter the kitchen. Clifford had gone back to the scullery. Anthony was in the cellar, Sandy Bellows in the powder room, and Mrs. Smithings upstairs. Rosie was clearing up in the drawing room and Helen was wandering about downstairs with her phone.

"What did you do next?" he asked Helen when he returned to the table.

"I tried to get a signal from the drawing room. I asked Rosie where Mrs. Smithings had gone, and she said upstairs as she was complaining of a headache and needed to lie down."

"What was Rosie doing in the drawing room?"

"She was tidying up. She said she would be in shortly to serve the main course. I lingered awhile as there was a big blaze in the fireplace. It was nice and warm, unlike in here." Helen rubbed her arms. "It's a bit chilly, isn't it?"

The others agreed.

"Was Rosie with you the whole time?"

"Yes."

At that moment, Mrs. Smithings entered, looking even paler than usual.

"How is your headache, Mrs. Smithings?" Rex asked.

"Oh, that. Well, I had rather forgotten about it under the circumstances. Mrs. Bellows is ready to serve the Dover sole if anyone still has an appetite."

"Aye, let's not let good food go to waste." Rex had not eaten much at tea and had missed lunch altogether.

Charley appeared with the candlesticks, holding each by the base. "I wasn't sure how long you wanted me to babysit these," he told Rex, "so I took the liberty of bringing them in."

"Put them down on the sideboard where I can keep an eye on them, Charley."

"And what do you propose doing with those candlesticks?" Mrs. Smithings demanded.

"I'll dust them for prints after dinner. One of them may have been used for the murder of Miriam Greenbaum."

"Why do you think that?" Wanda asked, her eyes round with ghoulish excitement.

"Because the candlesticks were standing next to the tureen on the kitchen table. It's possible that the person who struck Miriam picked up the BlackBerry after Miriam dropped it, and then threw it into the soup when he or she was replacing the candlestick on the table. I'll need talcum powder and clear tape."

"I have some Yardley rose-scented talc in my room," Yvette offered. "Will that do?"

"That will do grand, lass."

A discussion about forensics ensued as Mrs. Smithings removed Ms. Greenbaum's place setting and chair. The cook prepared the plates at the heating trays on the oak sideboard, and Rosie served the guests. No one but Charley appeared to notice the dog bolt through the door and burrow beneath the tablecloth at Rex's feet, panting and drooling as it thumped its tail on the rug. Staying Yvette's arm before she could put her fork to her lips, the medic surreptitiously offered the dog a piece of fish from his plate, and this went down a treat.

"I'm not sure how I feel about us using the poor wee animal as a dog taster," Rex murmured, dropping some of his own fish on a saucer and placing it on the floor, "but it's no a bad idea at that."

His Dover sole having passed the test, Rex plunged his fork into the cream and mushroom sauce. Clifford, hiccupping, stumbled into the room and placed a log on the fire.

"That's much better," Helen approved.

Conversation turned to the snow and to when the phones might become operable again. Each guest made an effort to affect an air of normalcy. Everyone at the hotel was at present gathered in one room, and Rex looked at each person in turn, wondering who among them was guilty. Supervised by Mrs. Smithings, Rosie and the cook removed the heating trays, and they left.

He continued observing and analyzing through dessert, knowing he would have to launch a full investigation now that the cat was out of the bag. If the innocent had believed the old man died of ill health, their suspicions must now be aroused by Ms. Greenbaum's demise.

He had to discover the identity of the culprit before someone else was murdered. Rex all but choked on his cheese and biscuits: a third murder?

"A wee bit more of that claret to wash down this delicious cheddar," he said to Anthony. He had watched Smart uncork the bottle and was sure the wine wasn't contaminated.

Helen smiled beside him, picking at her food. "I admire your appetite."

"I hope it doesna make me appear insensitive, but eating helps me think. I always have a big breakfast before court."

Wanda held out her glass for a refill. "I found I was putting on weight from my depression so now I take pills to curb my appetite."

"You're practically anorexic!" Yvette observed. "I don't think you have to worry."

Wanda preened a bit, and the women departed on a discussion about diets. The mood lifted as the guests were temporarily distracted from the specter of evil haunting the manor. Anthony, revived by food and drink, added his two-pence worth on health food.

When the guests finally left the dining room, seeming reluctant to split up one from the other, Rex remained at table. He gathered up the name cards and grouped those belonging to the persons present in the drawing room at the time of Lawdry's death. These included all but Yvette and Charley Perkins, who had been upstairs in their suite. He then isolated the cards of those who'd remained at table when Ms. Greenbaum fell to the cellar floor. Only Patrick and Wanda had been with him. These two could not have been directly involved in Miriam's death.

Rex wished Helen had not taken the phone call and left the room, so he could eliminate her as well.

———

Rex reviewed the timeline according to what he'd been told. When Clifford took the firewood to the cellar, the rest of the staff had been in the kitchen. By the time he returned, only the cook was there. Anthony passed her in the corridor on his way to the kitchen. Ms. Greenbaum arrived thereafter. Helen searched for Mrs. Smithings downstairs and spoke to Rosie in the drawing room. Clifford stayed in the scullery after depositing the wood in the cellar. Rex came to the same conclusion as before: One of them had to be lying.

When he joined the guests in the drawing room with the candlesticks, Rosie was serving coffee. Wanda, Charley, and Yvette sat by one of the tall windows, playing a subdued game of cards. Helen occupied the fourth chair at the card table.

"Want to join us in a game of crazy eights?" Charley asked him.

"I'll pass, thank you though."

Helen looked up from her knitting. Even at this distance, Rex noticed the fear in her eyes. Now that the adrenaline had worn off, she must be confronting the stark reality of Ms. Greenbaum's death. As though reading his thoughts, she said, "It feels strange and empty without Miriam here."

Charley shuffled the pack and began dealing between the three players.

"I can't concentrate," Yvette said, pushing away her five cards as Charley placed the undealt stock face down on the table.

"When are you going to test the candlesticks?" Wanda asked Rex.

"I want everyone here first. Mrs. Bellows is still finishing up in the kitchen." He accepted a cup of coffee from Rosie and helped himself to two sugar lumps from the black lacquer tray.

Coffee was just what he needed. He was finding it hard to stay awake after taking the overnight Edinburgh to London rail service, traveling ninety minutes from Victoria Station to Eastbourne, and waiting over an hour for a train to Swanmere. Yet, much as he longed to crawl into his bed upstairs, he had two murders to mull over.

"Ring Around the Rosie," Charley chanted, encircling the girl's waist with his arm as she approached the card table.

"Watch out, I'll drop the tray!" Laughing, she refilled his cup. "Would you like some more coffee?" she asked Yvette.

"No, thank you very much," the newlywed replied with icy dignity, staring furiously at Charley.

"Not for me, thanks, Rosie." Helen glanced over at Charley. "You're in high spirits," she said, knitting needles clicking.

It sounded like a reproach to Rex, though the delivery was neutral enough.

"What's the point in wallowing in doom and gloom? Like that pair over there," he added under his breath, just loud enough that Rex heard.

Rex glanced to the other side of the room where Anthony sprawled despondently in his usual armchair by the fire, which had petered out, leaving a mound of cooling ash in the grate.

Rex stepped toward him, careful not to spill his coffee. "You look a wee bit under the weather, Anthony."

"I'm going to have nightmares tonight. I keep seeing her staring eyes. It's as though she's reproaching me."

"I have something you can take to help you sleep," Patrick said in soothing tones. "It's all-natural and quite safe."

"I'm glad you never saw her," Anthony told his partner.

"Aye, but the best thing we can do now is find out who did it. Yvette, are you ready with that talcum powder?" Rex gave Rosie instructions as to the other items he needed, including the tray she was holding, which he asked her to clean top and bottom.

Lowering himself onto a tapestry footstool in front of the fire, he asked Anthony to describe the scene at tea the previous afternoon. He thought it might help get Anthony's mind off Miriam and provide additional information while they waited to see what clues, if any, the candlesticks revealed.

"The old man served himself coffee by mistake," Anthony recounted. "He was already sitting down and since I was going to get more tea for myself, I offered to get him some as well. We were discussing how bad sugar was for the health, and he mentioned wearing dentures from eating too much of it. I noticed he was spooning the icing out of his tart. Why are you asking? Has this anything to do with Miriam?"

Rex stirred his coffee. "Possibly."

"You're suggesting that Lawdry was murdered too, aren't you?"

"We don't know for sure."

A brief chat with each of the other guests who had been present at tea corroborated Anthony's account and that of Patrick earlier that day. All the guests had been in the drawing room except Charley and Yvette Perkins. Lawdry helped himself to the coffee and iced tart. Anthony was on his way back from the table with Lawdry's cup of tea when the old man succumbed to a seizure. Patrick came to his assistance first. Anthony left to get Charley from the honeymoon suite. By the time the medic reached the old man, he was dead.

As Rex recalled, the cook had mentioned Anthony and Miriam coming into the kitchen on occasion, but anyone could have snuck in, just as Clifford had managed to smuggle the sherry and dog past her. And yet, if someone had tampered with the tart, how could that person have known whose plate it would end up on? Just as perplexing, the old man didn't appear to have any personal connection to Ms. Greenbaum. Perhaps a dusting of the candlesticks would produce the necessary leads.

"Rosie, would you be kind enough to fetch the rest of the staff?"

With everyone in attendance, Rex proceeded to sprinkle the talc from the tin of Yardley's over one of the candlesticks. A sweet smell of rose tickled his nostrils.

"What a lovely fragrance," Helen said to Yvette. "I'll have to get some."

Taking extreme care, Rex blew away at the powder until it adhered only to where oil had been left by someone's fingers. He then taped over the prints, which he peeled off and placed on the upturned black lacquer tray. Distinct patterns of arches, loops and whorls stood out clearly before him.

"Well, I never," Charley said.

Mrs. Smithings bent over the tray. "Reginald, you never cease to astound me."

Rex asked Clifford, Anthony and Charley to step forward. "Since each of you carried at least one of the candlesticks, I'm going to start with you. All your prints should be here. Then we can identify who else's prints are present."

"Whaaa—what are you doing?" Clifford asked as Rex reached for his hand and attempted to position one of his fingers on Mrs. Smithings' stamp pad.

"The police used this technique in the late 1880s—that's about a decade before this manor was built. They coated a person's fingertips with ink, like so … and deposited the prints on white paper." Using gentle pressure, Rex rolled the old man's inked finger on the blank inside of a Christmas card. "This way, they could match up prints with the patterns of lines found at the crime scene."

"I didn't do nothin'," Clifford protested.

"I just want to eliminate your prints since you carried the candlesticks from the scullery."

"But if he committed the murder, the prints won't prove anything," Anthony pointed out. "Same goes for me and Charley."

Rex gave Clifford a damp rag to wipe off his fingers. "I realize that. What will be interesting is if we find a fourth set of prints." He compared Clifford's card to the samples on the tray and found matches. "I saw a box of Tiddlywinks somewhere. Could someone bring it to me?"

Patrick handed it to him. Rex extracted yellow discs and placed them above Clifford's prints on the tray. He repeated the inking procedure with Anthony, color-coding his prints with red discs, and Charley's with blue. All the prints on the tray were now accounted for. No fourth set of prints existed.

Rex sprinkled the second candlestick with talc and found no prints on it, not even Clifford's, even though he'd carried both candlesticks into the kitchen. His prints appeared only on the first, along with Anthony's and Charley's, who had both taken it down to the cellar. As these constituted the only sets on the tray, it was unnecessary to fingerprint anybody else.

The experiment availed nothing except to prove that the second candlestick tested was the murder weapon, the killer having taken care to wipe it clean.

"And what other magic tricks do you have up your sleeve, Reginald?" Mrs. Smithings asked.

"I'd like to check the rooms upstairs, if I may."

"The guest suites? And why, pray?"

Rex intercepted a startled look from Yvette to her husband. "Ms. Greenbaum's manuscript is missing from its file. It might lead us to the perpetrator." Rex checked his watch, calculating the time difference with the States. "And I'd like to contact her office if possible to notify someone of her death before tomorrow, as the agency is probably closed on Christmas Eve. The manuscript had the phone number on the first page."

"The phones are out," Helen reminded him.

"With any luck they'll be restored."

"Perhaps it's in her room," Mrs. Smithings said.

"I looked, and in any case she was working on it just before she went in to dinner." Rex glanced around the circle of guests and staff. "I understand what an imposition this might be, but if you would permit me to search all your rooms, it might speed up proceedings when the police finally get here."

"I don't mind," Patrick said. "It would provide a diversion. There's not much else to do."

"A real-life game of Cluedo might be fun," Charley agreed. "Was it Clifford in the kitchen with the candlestick, or—"

"Look 'ere!" Clifford interrupted, bristling with impotent drunken ire.

"Just kidding, mate." Charley turned to Rex. "Since you wasn't here when poor old Henry croaked, or in the kitchen when Miriam got whacked with the candlestick, you're the only one in the clear and the only one we could trust to check our rooms. Just don't tell anyone what you find in ours," he added with a chuckle.

"I'll be the soul of discretion," Rex assured them all. "In the meantime, I'm going to appoint three groups to search downstairs: Charley, Helen, and Mrs. Smithings will form the first group; Anthony, Wanda, and Clifford, the second; Patrick, Yvette, and Rosie, the third. Mrs. Bellows will come with me."

He thought the female residents would feel less of a sense of violation if he took a woman with him while he snooped through their personal effects. "May I trouble you for a pair of rubber gloves?" he asked the cook. Her hands were almost as big as his.

"And what exactly are we looking for?" Mrs. Smithings demanded as the cook bustled out of the room.

"Ms. Greenbaum's manuscript and anything else remotely suspicious."

"Do we get a prize for the best find?" Helen joked.

"Aye, a kiss under the mistletoe from me."

Helen let out a delightful trill of laughter. "I'm game," she told him.

Rex was glad to see she had recovered her spirits.

"This isn't an Easter egg hunt, you know," Anthony reminded them. "Miriam is lying dead in the cellar."

Wanda humphed. "You weren't so concerned about her when she was alive."

"And I'll regret it to my dying day."

"That won't do her any good now," Charley said pragmatically. "You should just be grateful it's not you that got clobbered."

"I urge everyone to please be respectful of property," Mrs. Smithings shrilled. "And to put everything back exactly as you found it. Where shall we start?"

Rex divided the downstairs rooms between the three groups and coughed apologetically. "I'll need the keys for upstairs." He decided not to let everyone know he had a master key—it might prove a useful card up his sleeve later on.

"I'm sharing with Rosie," Mrs. Bellows said. "The room's unlocked. You'll not find much of mine there, except for the clothes I arrived in."

"I wouldn't want just anyone prying into my things," Rosie added. "But you seem like a decent sort of bloke and you are in the legal profession, which makes it all right, I suppose."

"My room's a mess," Wanda warned him, handing over her key.

"I know this may seem highly irregular," Rex said, "but we must get to the bottom of this for everyone's peace of mind."

For the peace of mind of the innocent, at any rate, he thought wryly; for the culprit it would be a different matter.

SIX

EVEN IF HE FOUND nothing conclusive, Rex reasoned that a search of the guest rooms might provide him with insightful character clues. Much could be revealed by a person's possessions. As he exited the drawing room, the dog bolted after him from the direction of the kitchen.

"What's that dog doing here?" Mrs. Smithings demanded, her displeasure tightening the angles of her face. "I thought when I first heard about it that it was a joke."

Clifford shuffled forward. "Ee got loose. 'Ere, boy!"

"Pets are not permitted in the establishment. Clifford, you of all people should know better. Whose dog is it anyway?"

"It's mine," Rex confessed. "At least temporarily. I found it by the train station, and Clifford is being kind enough to keep it in the scullery until we decide what to do with it."

"Well, it's not in the scullery now, is it?" Mrs. Smithings asked rhetorically. "And it's not even a pedigree!"

The puppy yapped, jumping up at Rex's feet, waiting for him to produce a treat from his pocket. "I'm sorry it's no a corgi," he said.

She put a hand to her temple. "Such a trying noise! As soon as Clifford has finished his part in the search, he must take that—that *dog* back to the scullery and keep it there."

Rosie crouched by the puppy and fed it a sugar lump while Mrs. Smithings swept down the hallway with Charley and Helen in tow to perform their part of the search.

Sticking his thumbs in his ears, Charley wiggled his fingers behind the proprietor's back. Helen threw Rex an amused smile as Mrs. Smithings disappeared into the parlor-office.

"All right, Mrs. Bellows," Rex said. "Are you ready?"

The puppy made to follow Rosie as she joined Yvette and Patrick, assigned the library, kitchen, and scullery—then changed its mind and trailed Rex up the stairs.

Feeling like a clumsy cat burglar in his latex gloves, borrowed from Mrs. Bellows, Rex started with the rooms in the west wing. Disregarding basic articles of clothing and hygiene, he wrote down a summary of items in his notebook:

Patrick Vance (#1): Homebrewed valerian root sleep aid, blank sketchbook, leather manicure set.

Anthony Smart (#2): Rogaine, vitamin supplements, library edition of The Razor's Edge *by Somerset Maugham, half-empty bottle of Courvoisier brandy stowed away in a tallboy.*

Working his way down the corridor, he skipped his own room and crossed the landing to the east wing. Unlike Patrick and Anthony's suite, Wanda's room looked like a grenade had exploded, dispersing clothes, purses, and shoes in every direction.

"Lordie," Mrs. Bellows exclaimed when she saw the crammed contents of the medicine cabinet.

Rex made a brief inventory of the arsenal of lethal-sounding products designed to fight wrinkles, defend against free radical damage, and attack excess pounds, and added: *Incense tapers (patchouli), 2 issues of* Cosmopolitan, *fitness magazines, photo album, key labeled "Master" in bedside drawer.*

That, he thought triumphantly, was how she had been able to get into number four to pay the dead Mr. Lawdry a visit.

Next came Helen's bedroom. Rex felt a ripple of voyeuristic anticipation and found himself experiencing a sense of relief that, though her room had a lived-in look, it in no way resembled the chaos residing in Wanda's.

Helen d'Arcy (#6): Knitting needles, sundry balls of wool, textbook on child psychology, unfinished letter to "Clive." What was this? He read it to find out.

"*…I'm sorry I couldn't go skiing with you in Aviemore, but I felt we needed some time apart. I'm not the person you think I am…*"

Mrs. Bellows tut-tutted as Rex perused the private letter.

"Desperate times call for desperate measures," he told her. Where had he heard that before? "Well, no sign of the manuscript so far."

He locked the door and proceeded to the last occupied guest suite. "Lucky number seven," he said, opening the door to the honeymoon suite. "Stay," he commanded the dog, which paid no attention and shot in between his feet.

Unlike the other suites, where two adjoining rooms shared a bath, this was a double room dominated by a canopy bed draped in rumpled yellow floral chintz. A teddy bear stared out from the snowy starched pillows. Picking it up, Rex saw it was zippered at the back, the inside lined with red quilted satin. Under Mrs. Bellow's baleful eye, he tipped it over the bedspread, and an oval cameo brooch tumbled out from among the silky folds of a negligee.

Upon closer examination, he found that the brooch was in fact a locket containing a worn engraving, which he couldn't make out, even when he held it under the bedside lamp. He would need his magnifying glass. The cook scowled at him when he pocketed it.

"Evidence," he explained, scribbling in his notebook.

Mr. & Mrs. Perkins (#7): Soft toy containing ivory cameo brooch approx. 5 by 4 cm with gold grapevine border; intact packet of oral contraceptive; massage oil; book entitled Hot Sex for Cool Couples.

"Oooh, I like the sound of that," Mrs. Bellows said when she saw it on the bedside table. "Wonder if they've discovered something new since me and the old man got wed. After thirty-five years I'd as soon have a cup of tea."

"Perhaps you could get a copy from the local library. Now then, on to the staff accommodation," Rex directed, letting her lead the way down the corridor. He whistled to the puppy to follow.

"Mrs. Smithings' is this door here," the cook informed him. "Best keep the dog out."

Facing south over the garden, the suite consisted of a sitting room, bedroom, and bath. Unlike the parlor-office downstairs, it was almost Spartan in its furnishing. The few pieces in the rooms, however, were choice, including a cherry wood chest of drawers and an intricately carved armoire, which Rex opened. An aroma of mothballs and lavender enshrouded the black dresses that Mrs. Smithings favored.

Next, he lifted the lid of a colored glass jewellery box on the dressing table. "I thought Mrs. Smithings owned a great many jewels," he commented to the cook, his voice seeming to echo in the absolute silence of the room.

"Most are kept in a safe downstairs."

A framed sepia photograph of Mrs. Smithings' late husband, one booted foot resting on a felled elephant, stood on the mantelpiece beside a marble and ormolu clock pointing to ten on the hour. The blue Victorian tiles decorated with white swans surrounding the fireplace were cracked. It must cost a good deal of money to maintain this drafty old place, Rex reflected.

Another photograph, this one of her son at the officer cadets' Passing Out Parade at Sandhurst took pride of place by her bedside. A framed newspaper cutting headlined "Troop Commander Captain Rodney Smithings, Royal Artillery, Killed by RPG in Iraq" hung on the wall among a series of botanical watercolors.

Feeling here more than elsewhere that he was intruding, Rex concluded his tour of the owner's rooms and succinctly noted: *Mrs. Smithings' suite: Jewellery box containing one pair of pearl earrings; Rodney memorabilia; painkillers for rheumatoid arthritis.*

"You didn't write much," Mrs. Bellows observed.

"Didn't find much."

The cook eased the door shut behind them and glanced at her watch. "It's a quarter to ten. Just Rosie's room now, thank goodness—I'm ready for bed."

Rex checked his own watch. "The clock on Mrs. Smithings' mantelpiece must be fast."

Mrs. Bellows lit the wall sconces and turned into a corridor skirting the east wall of the house. Behind a door at the end of the corridor rose a flight of narrow stairs, and Rex suddenly recalled the way to his old attic room through what he used to pretend was a secret passage.

A warren of erstwhile servants' rooms burrowed under the roof.

"Most of the rooms are used for storage," Mrs. Bellows explained.

When Rex opened a door upon a dark space filled with sports equipment and a broken rocking horse, a squeaking horde of hump-backed shapes scurried away across the floorboards. One ran onto his foot and up his pant leg. Mrs. Bellows shrieked. Grabbing a broom, he swept the rat into the air and leaped out the door, slamming it shut.

"Now, why did you have to go in there for?" the cook asked, her bosom heaving with emotion. "Clifford's supposed to keep the rats under control. They'll gnaw away at the timber until there's nothing left." Whisking the broom from his hands, she shielded herself with it and hastened down the corridor.

Rosie's room was off to the left. Squeezing through the door to the sloping-walled room, Rex bumped his head and careened into a walnut chest of drawers, sending a pile of Mills & Boon novels toppling onto the carpet. Above one of the twin beds hung a series of photos and an advent calendar sparkling with glitter. That day's paper window remained closed. As a boy, Rex couldn't wait to open the windows, each morning awaking in growing anticipation of ever bigger Christmas scenes.

"That's Rosie's bed," Mrs. Bellows said. "No room to swing a cat in here, is there?"

Rex came to from his memories. "What happened to Rosie's sister? I heard she used to work here."

"Oh, it was a terrible tragedy. They were like two peas in a pod." Mrs. Bellows lifted a corner of her apron and blotted her eyes. "You'll have to forgive me—I get all teary when I think about it."

"An illness?" Rex probed.

"Train wreck." She peeked through the twill drapes on the dormer window. "The snow's eased up at last."

"Good. I'll take the dog out for a quick walk before bed. Which reminds me, where is the wee devil?"

"He must still be downstairs."

After poking his head round the bathroom door in the corridor, Rex flipped to a fresh page in his notebook.

Rosie Porter (attic room): Romance novels, advent calendar, several photos of self.

He thought this quite narcissistic. Thanking the cook for her assistance, he made his way back down the narrow stairs, calling to the dog at intervals. He stopped by his room and with the aid of his magnifying glass deciphered the inscription inside the brooch before returning it to the honeymoon suite. It was only when he was halfway down the main stairway that the impact of what he had copied suddenly hit him.

With a tingly feeling that he might be on to something, he opened the guest book on the tripod table in the foyer and scanned the page until he found Lawdry's entry: *Henry D. Lawdry, The Paddocks, Hillcrest, Surrey.*

Rex compared the initials to the engraving from the locket. *To my beloved girl—Eternally Yours, H.D.L.*

What was a brooch inscribed with the dead man's initials doing hidden away in the Perkins' suite?

SEVEN

REX WROTE *R.I.P.* AFTER Lawdry's name in the guest book, and did the same after Ms. Greenbaum's, hoping he would not have to write these letters again during his stay at Swanmere Manor—and that they would not be written after his name for a long time to come.

The remainder of the household sat in the drawing room cradling mugs of cocoa, with the exception of Mrs. Smithings, who dryly asked permission to retire to her rooms. Mrs. Bellows and Rosie then excused themselves, saying they had to be up early. A chill pervaded the room, and Rex voiced his surprise at finding the fire unlit. Wanda told him about the discovery of a pile of embers, possibly belonging to the lost manuscript.

"We didn't want to disturb anything until you came back," Anthony said. "There are a few scraps of paper with letters on them."

"Well, let's get to work." Rex declined the cocoa Helen offered him. "Not right now, hen," he said, using the Scottish endearment, "but thanks anyway."

"Another time when you're less busy?"

His gaze met her blue eyes. "Aye, I'd like that." Then turning to Yvette, he asked, "Do you have a pair of tweezers?"

Following her out to the hall, he showed her the words he had copied from the locket. Yvette went pale. "H.D.L.—Henry D. Lawdry, if I'm not mistaken …"

At last she said, "I know how it looks, but I didn't steal the brooch. When Henry died, Charley told me to hide it so people wouldn't ask questions."

"How did you come by it?"

"Henry said I reminded him of his daughter and he wanted me to have it. Anthony told me it was worth over five hundred pounds and I should keep it in Mrs. Smithings' safe."

"So Anthony Smart knew about the brooch, and yet you said you didn't want anyone asking questions."

"That was after Henry died. Charley doesn't know I asked Anthony to appraise it. I was just curious as to its value."

"Who else knows Mr. Lawdry made you a gift of the brooch?"

"You don't believe me," Yvette accused. "You think I stole it!"

"Calm down, lass. I don't know what to think at present—about any of this."

"That's probably why Charley said to hide it, so people wouldn't jump to the wrong conclusions!"

Rex was puzzled that her husband hadn't mentioned the brooch when he told him about the cyanide. After all, he had asked Charley to tell him everything he knew about Lawdry. He would have to confront him about it. In the meantime, there was the matter of the manuscript. "If you're not too cross with me, could you fetch those tweezers?" he asked Yvette.

Pouting, she flounced off in the direction of the stairs. Rex gave a deep sigh. It had been a long day, and there was still work to do. If he could confirm the manuscript in the fireplace was the one Ms. Greenbaum had been working on—one she would never burn herself—it would suggest someone had an axe to grind.

Who under this roof could have bludgeoned the literary agent and poisoned a crippled old man?

Certainly, the murders were the work of a cunning mind: the first made to appear as though by natural causes, the second devised to look like an accident. Rex felt he might never get to the bottom of it, and yet try he must for Mrs. Smithings' and his mother's sake.

———

"Here you go," Yvette said, thrusting the tweezers into his hand.

Hitching up his trousers, Rex squatted by the fireplace and, with the care and precision of a surgeon, removed the charred scraps of paper and laid them out on cardboard. Delicate as moth wings, they were apt to fly away or else disintegrate at the slightest draft. "Could someone please close the doors?" he asked, shielding the fragments with his hand.

He scrutinized the remaining typeface on the scraps. The digit "one" appeared, followed by a space and the letters "Qa"—the rest of the word consumed by fire. All the Q words he could think of were followed by "u". Quantity, quarter, quick, quiet, quirk, quorum.

"Patrick, could you look for a dictionary in the library and see if there are any words beginning 'Qa'?" he asked.

The young artist returned within minutes holding a battered hardcover book with gold lettering. "According to the *Concise*

Oxford Dictionary, the only entries for "Q" are words beginning "qu" unless you count the abbreviations *q.v.* and *qy*."

"Well, blow me," Charley said. "I never realized every word in the English language beginning with 'q' started 'qu'."

"An encyclopedia might be more help," Anthony suggested. "It could be a foreign word like Qadhafi, the Libyan colonel."

"I couldn't find any other reference books. Is it important?"

"That remains to be seen," Rex murmured, sifting through the remaining fragments. One scrap revealed the letters "-yney" and "–IA". An abbreviation for Missing In Action or Central Intelligence Bureau? "I wish I had more to go on."

Patrick examined the evidence. "It must be the manuscript. I wonder who tried to burn it."

"Someone who didn't like Miriam," Helen speculated.

"None of us liked Miriam," Wanda said.

"No doubt the author kept a copy, but all Miriam's notes and comments have gone up in smoke—and she worked so hard on that biography."

Trust Helen to come up with a sensible and understanding view of the situation, Rex thought, finding more and more to like about her. "Did anybody come across anything else of interest?" he asked the group, determined to keep on track in spite of the heart flutters she inspired in him.

"Just a mouldy collection of stuffed wildlife in a glass case in the library," Yvette said.

"Specimens of hares, kingfishers, ducks, moorhens—that sort of thing," Patrick elaborated.

"Aye, those would be from Rodney Smithings' hunting days."

"Can we be of further assistance?" Anthony asked.

Rex glanced up from making entries in his notebook. "I don't think so, but thanks for all your help."

"Are we any closer to catching the killer?"

"Maybe." Rex stood up and flexed the cramps out of his legs. "I think I'll take the dog out for some fresh air—if I can find him."

"Clifford took him into the scullery," Anthony informed Rex. "The old man's asleep in a chair, snoring loud enough to wake the dead." He paused, then said, "Sorry, didn't mean it like that."

"I'm surprised he's not out cold after all the sherry he knocked back," Rex remarked. "But I'm glad he's sleeping. It wouldna be safe for him to walk back to the lodge in this weather."

Wanda approached with a twig of mistletoe. "Ta-da! I'm claiming my kiss. After all, I was the one who found the manuscript in the fireplace."

Closing her eyes, she puckered her lips, which wrinkled in an unappealing way. Rex knew he must kiss her on the mouth or risk offending her. Stooping, he planted a brief kiss on her lips, whereupon she giggled. "Oooh, you do have ticklish whiskers, Rex."

He winked at Helen who was watching with good-natured amusement, then drew Wanda aside. "I found a master key in your bedside drawer. Did Mrs. Smithings give it to you?"

A flicker crossed Wanda's immaculately made up face. "No, Rosie left it in the door this morning when she was making up my room. I meant to give it back."

"Well, perhaps you should before the girl gets into trouble."

"I know—I keep forgetting."

"May I ask what you were doing in Mr. Lawdry's room earlier?"

"I—I just wanted to pay my respects."

"I see," Rex said, unconvinced.

Wanda turned away before he could ask her anything else about her foray into the dead man's room. "I don't suppose you still want to do my hair?" she asked Patrick, pulling a hand through her dark locks and examining the ends.

Patrick glanced over at Anthony.

"Go ahead," his partner said. "I'm going to take a long hot soak in a sudsy bath with a book and a snifter of brandy. I probably won't surface for hours."

Helen began collecting the empty mugs of cocoa. "At least it's not snowing now." Covering her mouth, she yawned. "I'd best get off to bed. I'm dead on my feet."

"Bolt your doors," Rex warned everyone as they traipsed out of the drawing room. "Charley, a word?"

Yvette paused too.

"I'll follow you up," her husband told her.

Wanda held back briefly and eyed the newlyweds with a look of suspicion.

Charley parked himself on a sofa and lit a cigarette. "Should we go and check the lodge while Clifford's asleep?"

Rex took out his pipe. With the others absent, he felt he could smoke with impunity. Charley offered him his box of hotel matches.

"Even if we could get over there, I don't think it's necessary," Rex replied. "I believe we can eliminate Clifford from our list of suspects."

"Why?"

"For one thing, he's not dexterous enough to have interfered with the iced tarts."

"True. His hands are all gnarled up."

"For another, I don't see what motive he could have for murdering Miriam Greenbaum. She was the only person who tipped him. In any case, he was totally sozzled."

"He could've hit her in a drunken rage."

"Clifford wasn't angry when I saw him—he was scared out of his wits, terrified Mrs. Smithings would find out about the sherry."

"So we strike him off our list?"

"Aye, for now. And I'd like to be able to strike you off the list too. I don't know if Yvette told you, but I found a cameo brooch in your suite."

"Yeah, but she said she explained why I told her to hide it."

"I need more convincing, lad."

Charley blew out a circle of smoke. "The old man was fond of my wife, they played Tiddlywinks together. When he kicked the bucket, I thought suspicion might fall on her if it came out that his death wasn't from natural causes. Everyone knew he was very wealthy."

"Anthony found out about the brooch."

"Yeah, well Yvette can't keep her mouth shut, can she?"

Rex sucked on his pipe, pursuing a line of thought. He poked the stem in Charley's direction. "You see, the fact of Mr. Lawdry giving your wife the brooch puts a slightly different complexion on things. It may indicate, for instance, that he was contemplating his end. Maybe he didna want to die alone at home."

"If he'd wanted to top himself, he had plenty of pills," Charley countered. "And how would he have known where to find the cyanide, unless he brought some with him? Also, if he did poison himself, why bother first wrapping the empty container in newspaper and throwing it out the back? You never met old Henry, but he was too feeble to go wandering about looking for a means to end his life."

"Aye," Rex conceded. "You make a good argument. But don't keep anything else from me. Even the most insignificant-seeming detail could be important."

Charley nodded sheepishly. "Sorry about that. You have my word."

Rex tapped out his ash in the fireplace. "Well, I'll be turning in now. Hopefully we'll make some progress tomorrow."

Leaving Charley, he headed toward the kitchen where, guided by the lamp in the scullery as by a lighthouse beacon, he navigated around the dim contours of furniture, catching the occasional gleam of a metal pot on a hook and the glint of a carving knife left out on a chopping board. Once in the scullery, he saw he was too late.

The pup had piddled on the floor. Rex found a mop and cleaned it up. Clifford never stirred.

"Barely out of nappies, eh?" Rex muttered to the sleeping dog. He would try to get to the village in the morning and put up a Dog Found announcement. He'd visit the constable too.

Wearily, he made his way up the main staircase and closed his bedroom door behind him with a dizzying sense of relief. He stripped out of his clothes and commenced his lengthy ablutions, ever mindful of his mother's admonishments never to skimp on his teeth. This was second only to keeping a bible by his bedside on her list of commandments—presumably in case he was taken ill in the night. There were others, and sometimes he recited them to help him fall asleep.

He threaded the towel back in its ring and set his alarm. Once tucked up in bed, he reviewed his notes. Aye, he thought, when he reached Wanda's list of personal items. Incense tapers—that was the fragrance he'd detected in Lawdry's room. But why light incense in there? Perhaps she had a morbid fascination with death, or perhaps she was on some sort of guilt trip. But Wanda couldn't have pushed Miriam down the steps. She and Patrick had been at table with him.

Miriam Greenbaum and Henry Lawdry... What connection existed between them? Lawdry's murder was premeditated—a certain amount of preparation must have gone into spiking the tart, whereas Miriam's was an opportunity killing. No one could have foreseen that she would be at the top of the cellar steps at a moment when there were no witnesses.

What if the connection was single guests, alone like himself? The thought accelerated his heartbeat.

What about the charred remnants from the fireplace? If someone had wanted Miriam's death to look like an accident, why burn the manuscript? There seemed no rhyme or reason to any of it.

After turning off the bedside lamp, Rex thrashed about until he found the perfect spot beneath the goosedown quilt, and willed himself to suspend thought of the murders. He hoped there would be porridge at breakfast, preferably Scots Quaker Oats with dollops of cream and brown sugar... With a contented sigh of anticipation, he began to relax, teetering on the brink of oblivion. It was no use.

The persistent and growing pressure on his bladder told him he would have to take care of business before there could be any chance of sleep. Huffing with resignation, he cast off the quilt and felt with his feet for his slippers as he reached out for the lamp switch.

An antique chamber pot sat invitingly on the chest of drawers. On further inspection, he found it contained *pot pourri*. Tempting as it was, he decided he would have to use the bathroom across the hall. Donning his blue and white striped flannel dressing gown, he slipped into the corridor illuminated by low-wattage wall sconces, and stiffened. A figure stood a few paces down the hall brandishing a fire poker.

"What in streuth's name are you doing with *that*?"

Anthony moved toward him swinging the poker as though participating in a fencing match. "It could be quite deadly, couldn't it? Solid iron," he said, hefting its weight.

"Stop right there." Much to his relief, Anthony did as requested. "Didn't mean to scare you."

"Aye, well you did look a wee bit menacing."

"I was just giving you a demonstration. For all I know, someone could jump out from a secret door in the wood panelling. Or from behind one of these hanging tapestries."

"There aren't any secret doors. I explored this whole place when I was a lad. Anyway, what are you doing out of your room at this hour?"

"I had to go to the men's room and decided to take some form of protection with me. I'd hate to be victim number three."

Rex tightened the belt on his cartoonish bathrobe, feeling a bit silly next to Anthony in his black-edged burgundy dressing gown. "You have your own bathroom, so why come out at all?"

"Patrick has indigestion. He's pretty much holed up in ours. It's all the curry and rich sauce he ate, not to mention the cocoa afterwards. I told him he'll end up clogging his arteries, but at his age they don't listen. What's your excuse for roaming the halls?"

"I have an irritable bladder."

"Could be the beginning of prostate trouble. You should get it checked."

"Aye, I might do that."

The men stood facing each other awkwardly, Rex reluctant to turn his back on the poker-wielding Anthony. "If it makes you feel better, I'll walk you back to your room and then borrow your poker, if I may," he suggested.

"Fair enough."

Rex escorted his nocturnal companion to the end of the corridor and returned armed. Having gained the men's bathroom, located across from Lawdry's room, he looked around the small space. No trace remained of anyone else's presence, unless Anthony was as fastidious as himself, which was quite possible, judging from his room. It was equally possible that Anthony had been on his way to, or coming back from, somewhere farther afield.

In any case, Rex thought, relieving himself; if someone *had* been murdered by a fire poker during the night, he would know whom to go to. It was too late to wake everyone now.

EIGHT

REX AWOKE TO A cold light pressing into the room around the edges of the drapes. Rubbing his eyes, he turned the clock to face himself. Almost nine. He must have slept through his alarm. Fifteen minutes later, showered and dressed, he stepped into the corridor. Helen was entering her room down the hall. "Morning," he called.

Turning around, she smiled, neat and fresh in blue slacks and a white cowl-neck sweater that showed off her bust line to advantage. "Going down to breakfast?" she asked.

"Aye," he said, ambling toward her, hands in pockets. "I slept late after all the excitement last night."

"I just had mine, otherwise I would join you."

"I didna want to kiss Wanda last night, you know," Rex confided in a hushed voice.

"I could tell. I have a few letters to write—if I ever get the opportunity to post them before next year—and then I'll be down."

Letters. He wondered if she was going to finish the one to Clive. "I made an interesting find yesterday evening while I was poking around in the attic," he said. "Skis. Old wooden ones, mind. And two pairs of lace-up boots. Fancy a trip down to the village?"

Helen looked intrigued. "I'm not that good a skier. I mean, I can stay up … Oh, but that would be amazing. Would we make it?"

"The sun's up, and from what I could see from my window, the snow looks compacted enough. One set of boots might fit you."

"Rex, you're a godsend. I would just love to get out for a while." She bit her lip guiltily. "Wanda's still in bed. She sometimes sleeps until ten …"

"Och, we'll be gone by then."

"Do you have business in the village?"

"Aye—a pint at the local pub."

Helen let out a little shriek of excitement. "You wicked man! Well, let me get those letters finished so I can bring them with me to post. Forty-five minutes, downstairs?"

"Meet me in the scullery. We'll put on our skis there and go the back way through the forest."

Rex continued down the landing toward the narrow arched window to check the weather from the east. As he passed the honeymoon suite, he heard muffled voices behind the door, Yvette sounding hysterical, and then Charley saying, "I thought we were going to wait until we had the money …"

"It was an accident."

"What are we going to do?"

"Nothing. Nobody need suspect anything."

"It'll come out eventually, and anyway you can't keep your mouth shut, Yvette."

"Sod you!"

"Well, it's true. I can't be cooped up forever…I'll go insane."

"We can sell the cameo…"

Rex leaned in toward the door, assuring himself that under different circumstances he would never presume to eavesdrop on a personal conversation—just as he would never normally read someone's private mail. Never.

Charley muttered something.

"That's murder, Charley!"

More murmuring, then Charley asked, "What d'you call what you did to Henry?…"

"…I see how you look at that slut, chatting her up…"

The voices grew closer and Rex decided it was time to make himself scarce. He would check the weather from downstairs. When he reached the foyer, he pulled his notebook from his pocket and scribbled down the ominous-sounding snippets of conversation he'd overheard. In the dining room, Anthony and Patrick sat at table reading crumpled newspapers.

"Three-day-old papers," Anthony complained over a bowl of muesli. "Though I don't know why I even bother reading the news anymore. How did that bungling American idiot ever get elected to a second term? They must put brainwashing chemicals into their Big Macs."

Patrick nursed a cup of black tea, a piece of dry toast half-eaten on his plate.

"Morning, Patrick. You seem a bit green around the gills." Rex gestured toward their newspapers. "Can you save me the crosswords if no one's done them yet?"

Mrs. Bellows bustled around the heating trays on the sideboard. "There's bacon and scrambled eggs, fried mushrooms and kippers," she told him. Patrick made a queasy sound at the mention of kippers. "I'll send Rosie in with more crumpets."

"That would be grand."

"Do you have any special requests?" the cook asked on her way out the French doors.

"Well, I do like porridge in the morning."

"I can make some."

"Don't trouble yourself today."

"I don't think Mrs. Bellows likes us very much this morning," Anthony remarked. "I never eat the fried stuff and Patrick is still feeling poorly from last night. Helen ate like a bird. You'd be doing us a favour if you polished off the kippers, Rex. They reek something horrible."

Rex helped himself to everything on offer and sat at the far end of the table so as not to offend the other two with his reeking fish.

Rosie rushed into the room. "Tea or coffee, Mr. Graves?" she asked Rex.

"Tea, thank you."

Anthony and Patrick rose from the table.

"Any special plans for the day?" he asked them.

Patrick shrugged. "More of the same. Watch TV, read, see what the weather does."

"Wait for another murder," Anthony added facetiously. "Are all guests present and accounted for this morning?"

"I can vouch for Helen and the Perkins."

"Speak of the devil," Anthony said as Charley and Yvette shambled into the room. "Well, enjoy your breakfast, all."

The honeymooners settled across from Rex. Yvette fidgeted with a strand of wool unraveling from her cardigan while her husband hummed and looked about him. "Where's Rosie?"

Yvette tensed up in her chair.

"She was here a minute ago. There's tea in the pot if you'd like some."

"Ta." Charley grabbed the pot and filled Yvette's cup.

Rex attempted to interpret the argument between the pair, but it was hard to focus with them right in front of him. "Did you sleep well?" he asked Yvette.

"Not very," she admitted, on the brink of tears. "It's my nerves. I feel all on edge."

"Aye, this is trying for all of us."

Charley rested a hand on her arm. "Can I get you some eggs and bacon, luv?"

Yvette nodded and blew her nose.

Rosie entered with a basket of hot crumpets and fresh tea. "Will anybody be wanting coffee?"

"No, we're all set, Rosie," Charley said from the sideboard, studiously avoiding her gaze.

Probably nothing was going on between Rosie and Charley, Rex surmised. At least, nothing beyond the mild flirtation that typically occurred between two attractive people of the opposite sex. Yet young people tended to get so jealous.

"What's on your schedule today?" Charley asked Rex, bringing two filled plates back to the table.

"Well, between us three, I might try to get down to the village."

"On the tennis rackets?" Charley chortled into his tea. "I saw you from the window yesterday. Maybe I could borrow them later?"

"What for?" Yvette asked.

"I'm getting claustrophobic, that's all. Don't know that I could make it all the way to Swanmere though," he told Rex. "It looks like hard work trampling about on those things."

"Aye, it is. My leg muscles are giving me gip today."

Yvette peppered her eggs. "Do you think the shops will be open?"

"On Christmas Eve? I doubt it. But the pub will be, I'm sure."

"Oh, he's going to the rub-a-dub-dub," Charley told Yvette with a nudge. "Can't keep a Scotsman from his whisky."

"Something like that," Rex said noncommittally, not wishing to divulge his more serious objective of meeting with the constable.

"I've got a Scots joke for you," Charley pursued.

"Aye, well I've probably heard it or some variation, but go ahead."

"Well, this Scotsman leaves the bar one night, and you can tell by the way he walks all zigzag-like that he's bloody elephant's."

"Trunk—drunk," Yvette interpreted. "Rhyming slang."

"So then he stumbles off the side of the road and falls asleep in the ditch. Not half an hour later, two gorgeous birds happen by. One says with a wink to the other, 'See yon sleeping Scotsman so strong an' handsome? I wonder if it's true there's nuffink beneath their kilts ... I say we take a butcher's—'

"Well, her friend's all for it, she's just as curious, so they creep up on the sleeping Scotsman and lift up his kilt inch by inch, slowly so as not to wake him, and beneath his skirt what do they see? No more and no less than his birthday suit, and a right bonny one at that. They marvel for a moment, all agog, and one says, 'Let's leave him a present before we go.' So they tie a blue silk ribbon on his crown jewels. Now the Scotsman wakes up some time later to answer the call of nature and, staggering behind a tree, lifts his kilt and gawks at what confronts him, he can't believe his eyes—he's got a standing election—"

"'Election'?" Rex questioned. "Och, aye, I get it now."

"And he says to himself, 'Oh, lad, I don't know where you've been, but I see you won first prize!'" Charley beamed all over his face.

"Ha, ha!" Yvette said, rolling her eyes.

Rex grinned. "I've heard the song a great many times, but the Cockney slang lends a whole new dimension. I thought when you mentioned a butcher that they planned to cut the thing off."

"Nah. A butcher's, as in butcher's hook. A look."

"Well, thanks for the entertainment, Charley. That'll do me for breakfast." Rex pushed back his plate and rose from the table. "See you both later."

"Don't be gone all day," Yvette said. "We have some activities planned for this afternoon."

"Aye? What sort of activities?"

"Charades and carol singing. We were practicing the other day. Helen has a beautiful voice."

"I'm a passable bass-baritone meself: 'God rest you, merry gentlemen, Let nothing you dismay!'" Rex roared, hand pressed to his chest. "But count me out of the charades."

"Spoilsport!"

"I'll keep score."

"Oh, all right. But do be there. It'll be fun."

Rex left the young couple to breakfast, thinking Yvette had perked up considerably for someone who'd accused her husband of murder only that morning. And Charley seemed his jovial self, though perhaps that Scots joke was overcompensating just a wee bit … Rex mulled over the words he'd overheard outside their suite:

"It was an accident, Charley … Nobody need suspect anything."

"It'll come out eventually … What d'you call what you did to Henry?"

None of it made much sense. Neither of them had been in the drawing room when Lawdry died, and Miriam's death could never be construed as an accident. Yet, tempted as Rex was to get to the bottom of it, he'd made plans with Helen. He would tackle Charley and Yvette individually when he got back from the village.

He crossed the kitchen, where Rosie was loading the dishwasher, and entered the scullery. Through the window, he saw Clifford muffled up in cap and scarf, chopping wood on a block. The puppy bounded about him, his mostly white body camouflaged by the snow, yelping with joy as Rex stepped over the threshold and plunged into the cold. At least the sun reflecting off the white powder lent an illusion of warmth—it would be pleasant enough with a coat on, he thought. The old man rested his axe against the wall and bid him good day.

Rex fed the dog the buttered crumpet he'd saved from the breakfast table and blew into his hands. "Clifford, I wonder if you could do me a favour. I saw skiing equipment in one of the attic rooms. Could you bring it down for me? Two pairs of everything."

"What would she say 'bout that?" the old man asked, jerking his head back at the house.

"Mrs. Smithings? I don't know, I haven't seen her. The stuff doesn't look like it's been used in decades. Is there any way you can bring it around the side of the house? I don't want everyone knowing I'm taking off for a couple of hours."

Clifford nodded, a crafty glint in his eyes. "There be a twitten the other side o' the hedge eh can bring 'em."

"Grand," Rex said. "What's a 'twitten'?"

"It be a path."

"I'll get my jacket and meet you back here. Oh, and you might want to put some rat poison down while you're at it. A gigantic rodent tried to run up my leg last night and Mrs. Bellows almost fainted. And then perhaps you should hide the poison," he added, thinking it safest not to leave anything lethal in temptation's way.

By the time he returned to the scullery with his jacket, Helen was waiting for him, looking fetching in a blue anorak and a pale blue bonnet that matched her eyes.

"It'll be an easy run down to the village," he said pulling on his gloves. "Coming back will be a different story."

She giggled. "Won't it be wonderful to get away for a while? I feel like I'm playing truant. I left Wanda a note in case she worries something happened to me."

"Well, try not to break a leg. Have you skied much?"

"Every year for the past four Christmases."

Clifford brought the skis to the door.

"My goodness, they look like they belong in a museum," Helen exclaimed, stepping outside. "Oooh, it's cold!"

"Aye, but they'll get us there and back."

Helen wrinkled her nose prettily. "Back. I'm not sure I like the sound of that. Couldn't we just stay in the village?"

"I'm not sure there *is* anywhere to stay down there. Anyway, I want to catch our killer, don't you?" He handed her the shorter skis and poles and placed the boots at her feet.

"I don't like the sound of the word 'killer' either. Strange, I never thought about it in quite those terms. I think my subconscious is holding onto the idea of a heart attack and a tripping accident." She sat on the doorstep lacing her boots. "I think these will do. I put on three pairs of socks—I have poor circulation."

Clifford was standing by with a pair of goggles. "Eh only found the one pair."

"I have my sunglasses," Helen told Rex. "You take the goggles. Thanks, Clifford. If I find a shop open, I'll bring you something back."

"The pub'll be open," the old man said hopefully.

Smiling, Rex clapped him on the back. "Did ye not have enough alcohol last night, Clifford?" He winked at Helen before adjusting the goggles, then snapped his boots onto the narrow skis and stuck his hands through the loops of the poles, which barely reached his hip. "Ready?" he asked Helen.

"As I'll ever be," she said, pushing herself off on her skis.

"Follow in my tracks. That'll make it easier."

The crisp snow held his weight as he half walked, half glided across the back lawns, making for the tree line where filigree frost shining among the pine branches resembled enchanted cobwebs. A glance over his shoulder assured him that Helen was keeping up with him.

"Watch out for stumps," he cautioned.

Once they were through the trees, the ground began to slope downward. Two miles away in the fold of the valley lay Swanmere, a cluster of white roofs and puffing chimneys, the village green transformed into a clean white handkerchief surrounded by tiny stone-wall shops and cottages. By the pond at the far end, Rex could just make out the Swanmere Arms aglow with fairy lights.

Helen slid to a stop beside him, panting slightly as she looked down the hill. "I wish I'd brought my camera, but I really didn't have anywhere to put it."

"Aye, it looks like a picture postcard. We'll be there in a jiffy."

He set off again, launching himself with his poles and bending his knees as the slope carried him past isolated copper beech trees and knots of sugar-sprinkled pines. The chill air whipped past his face, cutting through his slacks. Twisting around at the waist, he saw Helen follow after him in a stiff but competent style. The downhill momentum brought them to the edge of the village.

Cheeks flushed pink, Helen smiled from ear to ear. "That was exhilarating! Do you think there's a letter box on the way to the pub?"

"I need to make a quick detour first to see the constable. I can meet you at the pub if you like."

"I'll come with you. Where does he live?"

"Down this lane, according to Mrs. Bellows. She told me last night he was laid up with the flu." Rex stepped out of his skis. "It might be easier to walk. Just loosen your boots a wee bit."

Helen did as he suggested and he shouldered both pairs of skis, hoping against hope he wasn't going on a wild goose chase.

NINE

"HERE WE ARE," REX said, a quarter of a mile down a street lined on both sides with stationary, snowed-over cars. He knocked on the green door of a semi-detached Victorian, and a cheerful-looking woman in her mid-fifties answered. He stuck out his hand. "Mrs. Bowles? Rex Graves, QC. I've come to see your husband about an important matter. Sorry I couldna phone in advance, but the phones are out up at the Manor."

"Marjorie," the woman introduced herself, taking the proffered hand. "The phones are down here too. And you can't get through on a cell phone because people are resorting to those, and everyone calling because it's Christmas."

"This is my friend Helen d'Arcy, a guest at the hotel."

The women smiled at each other.

"Well, you best come in out of the cold. So you skied down? Just leave those on the mat and come on through. John has the flu but he's out of bed now."

She led them through the front room, past a narrow stairway and into the living room.

A television blared in front of the prostrate form of John Bowles wrapped in a blanket on a recliner, surrounded by the minty menthol smell of Vicks VapoRub. When he saw them, he picked up the TV clicker and turned down the volume on the soccer game. "Don't get too close," he warned through a clogged nose. "This one's a rotter."

"I hate to be disturbing you on Christmas Eve, especially when you're ill," Rex said, "but I understand Dahlia Smithings called you two days ago regarding a death at the hotel..."

John Bowles stared up at him in surprise, watery eyes streaming tears down his blotched face. "I don't think so."

Marjorie fluttered her hands. "She did call, John, but you were in bed. I told her you had the flu. She never said what it was about." While her husband gave vent to a phlegmy coughing fit, which he tried to confine to a wad of tissues, she poured two glasses of eggnog and set them down with a plate of mince pies on the coffee table. "Please sit down," she told the visitors. "When the snow started, John went out to help an elderly man who'd succumbed to hypothermia. That's when he caught cold."

The constable snorted mucous up his nose. "What's this about a death?" he asked Rex. "I feel like death warmed up myself. Margie, any chance of a toddy? Lots of lemon and honey and a dash of brandy. It's the only thing that really helps," he informed his visitors as his wife went into the kitchen. "The Vicks soothes the chest and clears the nose passages a bit, but the hot toddy works best."

Rex was beginning to wonder if their visit would serve any purpose other than to contaminate them with the flu germs that were almost palpable in the air. He imagined green gargoyles on legs winging around spewing virus.

"Will you be getting home for Hogmanay?" Mrs. Bowles called from the kitchen.

"Hopefully," Rex said, raising his voice.

"The train station said they would resume service on Boxing Day," the constable told him. "Oh, yes, tell me about the death up on the hill."

"Two deaths now," Rex said, lowering his voice again. "I suspect murder." Succinctly he filled John Bowles in on all the pertinent details. "Mrs. Smithings did, apparently, talk to the police and was given some advice from the doctor regarding the first case."

"That must be the ME over in Eastbourne. We've not even a GP here now since Peabody retired. Not big enough of a practice. Mrs. Bellows was his nurse."

Marjorie returned with the toddy, which Bowles proceeded to sip with fervor.

"I've written up an account for you," Rex told him. "I'm afraid I haven't got verra far in my investigations. I was hoping you could shed some light on the staff or perhaps be able to come up with some ideas from what I've told you."

The constable perused the brief statement. "No apparent motive for murdering the old man, I see—"

"Murder?" Marjorie said, shocked. "I thought it was a regular death."

Bowles cut her off with a glance. "So, he may have been murdered for the cameo," he resumed. "But if it's only worth 500 pounds... if that's an accurate evaluation. Now, that other murder—"

Marjorie gasped. "A second one?" Catching herself, she hastily served the visitors more eggnog before sitting down beside Helen on the sofa.

"Not a popular woman, this Ms. Greenbaum, as you describe her," the constable told Rex, "but that's hardly an adequate motive either. I wish I could help."

"What can you tell me about the people who work at the hotel?"

"I can tell you that Mrs. Smithings has become unhinged since her son's death."

"Quite natural," Helen said, "especially since he was her only son and she lost her husband shortly before that."

"True," the constable wheezed. "However, there is a history of mental illness on her side of the family. Her grandmother thought she was Lady Godiva, and one summer day rode stark naked on a white horse through the village and then went wading into the pond. Had some illusions she was a swan or something and almost drowned. She was put in an institution after that."

The clock on the mantelpiece chimed eleven. "Now that Rodney is dead, I don't know who will inherit the manor," Bowles concluded, honking into his tissues.

"Well, I think we've taken up enough of your time," Rex said, depositing his glass and rising from the sofa.

The constable waved his tissues. "Hold hard. That story about the drowning just reminded me of something. The old man that lives in the gatehouse was suspected of pushing his wife down a well, must be ten years ago now."

"Clifford Beadel?"

"That's right. He was found comatose. Nothing could be proved, though. His wife had an almost lethally high dose of alcohol in her as well. She used to be the housekeeper at the manor. That was when the colonel was still alive."

"Clifford is still fond of his drink. Well, I hope you feel better soon." Rex turned to Marjorie. "Thank you for your kind hospitality, Mrs. Bowles."

She showed them to the door. "That place is cursed if you ask me. Sandy Bellows is my sister-in-law's second cousin. She's not one for idle chatter, but she's worked at the manor going on seven years now and knows all the family history. The colonel pretty much ruined the family. A chinless wonder, that one, and—"

"Margie," her husband called, "It's time for my antibiotics. Achoo!"

"No rest for the wicked," Mrs. Bowles apologized. "Good luck to you. Two murders … Well, I never!"

Once he was back outside, Rex took a deep cleansing breath. The cold burned his lungs but it felt good. "I hope we didna catch anything in there," he commented to Helen as they trudged back down the lane, skis anchored on his shoulder.

"I know what you mean. I wanted to throw all the windows open. Remind me to take a double dose of vitamin C when we get back to the hotel. Slow down a little, will you?" she said with a laugh. "I don't have your long legs."

"Sorry, hen."

"Did you learn anything of interest back there?"

"There's something that struck a chord, but it's escaping me for now."

"That bit about Clifford makes one wonder, doesn't it? I mean, if he actually did murder his wife in a drunken stupor …"

"Aye. The drinking and pushing aspects are reminiscent of the circumstances surrounding Miriam's death. Clifford polished off half a decanter of sherry. Careful!" He grabbed Helen by the arm as she slipped on a slick patch of snow.

"Thanks," she said, recovering her balance. "Perhaps he was reliving the moment. If he passed out after pushing his wife down the well, he might not remember having done it when he came round. He may not have done it at all, but if he couldn't remember, he may have been plagued by guilt all these years. Then when the chance arose, he wanted to replay the event to see if he was capable."

"That's a convoluted theory, Helen."

"Perhaps, but it's amazing how the subconscious works."

"Aye, there's no denying that. I wish I could remember what it is that's niggling me."

They turned onto the village green.

"It's aggravating when that happens," Helen sympathized. "It happens to me more and more. A sign of approaching senility, I suppose. Think of something else while we have a drink—it might pop right into your head when you least expect it."

TEN

THE SWANMERE ARMS FACED the green and boasted a beer garden with trestle tables overlooking the pond, no doubt making it a pleasant spot in summer. Rex tried to envision it without snow on the tables. Frozen reeds fringed the ice-crusted surface of the pond, the few beech trees all but stripped of their leaves.

"Oh, look." Helen tugged his arm and pointed.

A pair of swans floating in the center of the pond created a lovers' heart with their graceful necks curved outward and heads bowed toward each other, orange beaks pointing to the water.

"Damn, I wish I *had* brought my camera. Aren't they beautiful? They're very loyal. They mate for life, you know."

"Aye, I think I heard that somewhere."

"And if they lose their mate, they go through a grieving process just as humans do."

"What sort of swans are they?"

"Mute swans, introduced to Britain in medieval times from the Black and Caspian Seas. All mute swans are owned by the Queen."

"You seem to know a lot about them." He turned toward the pub in pursuit of beer, gray snow crunching beneath his boots.

"I read up on them at the hotel. There are some nature books in the library."

Rex stacked the skis and poles around the side of the entrance and opened the half-glazed door, glad to feel the warmth of the interior. As he'd hoped, a fire crackled in a huge brick hearth. Bing Crosby crooned the lyrics of "White Christmas" from a speaker overhead.

"Oh, I love this song," Helen said.

The mahogany bar shaped in a horseshoe gleamed like glass, while red padded pews and brass fittings completed Rex's idea of how an English pub should look. He took a couple of seconds to savor the pungent smell of old beer wafting around the rafters strung with multicolored paper chains—and gave the Swanmere Arms an "A" rating.

A handful of people congregated around the dartboard at the far end of the bar, but this side was empty. Helen perched on a stool and unzipped her anorak.

"Merry Christmas," the barman said. "And what will you be having?"

"Vodka and tonic," Helen replied, unwinding the scarf from her neck. "And a packet of salt and vinegar crisps."

"Right you are, love. Sir?"

"Pint of Guinness."

"I thought you would order an Arran Blonde or a SkullSplitter," Helen joked.

"And how do you know so much about Scottish beer? Or have you been researching that as well?"

"I've been to Aviemore a few times with my on-off-again boy-friend and he likes to try the microbrews."

She must be referring to Clive. Rex contemplated the creamy white head at the top of his glass, wondering if she wanted to talk about it. Presumably she did or she wouldn't have brought him up. "*Sláinte*," he said, raising his glass and clinking her vodka and tonic.

"Bottoms up."

When they had taken a few long draughts, they both sighed in bliss.

"This is heaven," Helen remarked. "Just to be away from it all …"

"You mean your boyfriend?"

"Actually, I meant Wanda. But, yes, him too. I needed a break. Clive has been pushing for a decision I'm not ready to make. I'm pretty tied up with my job, which can get quite stressful on occasion, and when I get home I just want to relax and have time for myself. Does that sound selfish?"

"Not at all."

"Clive is a bit needy, a bit like Wanda, in fact. He teaches mathematics at the school. Not that he's boring or anything," Helen added a bit defensively, which Rex took as meaning he probably was.

"Wanda does seem to demand a lot of your time."

Helen pulled open her packet of crisps. "Well, we go back years. We were at university together, actually. She stole my boyfriend in our first year, the man she just divorced."

"Poetic justice."

"You can just imagine how angry I was at the time. I didn't speak to her for ages, avoided her in the Students' Union and everywhere I went. Fortunately for me, she dropped out. She married and I got on with my life, and then it didn't seem so important anymore. A year later we bumped into each other at a party. I suppose we were both a little drunk, and anyhow we just started laughing, and after that we were back to being best friends. I think it pissed Paul off."

"Is that what drove them apart?" Rex signaled to the barman for another round.

"A little, maybe. There's usually more than one factor involved. Wanda is basically insecure. I think that's why she made a play for Paul in the first place. Anyway, she was on the verge of a nervous breakdown after the divorce and needed a change of scene, somewhere peaceful where she could re-center herself, so I brought her here."

"Very understanding of you."

Helen dipped into her anorak pocket, opened a compact and repaired her lipstick. "What about you?" she asked, checking her handiwork in the mirror.

"Me? I'm probably not even as interesting as Mr. Algebraic Equation."

"Falsely modest," she said snapping her compact shut and jabbing him playfully in the shoulder.

"Tell me other things about myself." Rex was enjoying himself. The first Guinness had taken the edge off his thirst, the second was beginning to make him feel mellow.

"Well," Helen said matter-of-factly as she rolled back the sleeves of her white sweater. "The way you place objects so they don't touch one another … See—you moved the ashtray away, but not as far as the bar mat. You set the dish of peanuts out of the way of your notebook and left a space between it and your glass. You're a separatist, aloof, preferring your own company to that of others, and you shy away from physical contact."

"Not always."

"I'm speaking generalities. The interesting question for me is why?"

"Well, you've got me interested too. Why, doctor?"

"We'll get to that. I need to finish my character assessment first. You are intelligent, analytical—that's what makes you a good barrister—"

"How do you know I'm a good barrister?"

Unabashed, Helen told him that she had Googled him on Miriam's BlackBerry when he first arrived and found that he'd successfully defended the Crown in the vast majority of his cases.

"What else? I'm warming to me."

"You're very ethical. And respectful of women in an old-fashioned sort of way. Are you very close to your mother?"

"Aye. I lost my father when I was seven. My mother raised me with a blend of kindness and strict moral values. Whenever I misbehaved she beat me over the head with her bible."

"Women intimidate you."

"Argh, I wouldna say that."

"Well, maybe I'm reaching. But you're not a flirtatious man. I don't know what you think of me. I'd like to think you were attracted, but holding back for some reason." She rattled the ice in her vodka-tonic.

"There are plenty of reasons, Helen, not least of which being that I have two murders on my hands. But I find you bonnie enough, I'll give you that."

Helen blushed and stared into her glass. "But it's not going anywhere, is it?"

Rex felt some of his warm humor slip away. "I too have someone at home. She's a good woman—"

"You don't have to explain," Helen interrupted. "I knew you were ethical."

Rex bowed his head. Although the widow he'd been seeing in Edinburgh had gone overseas for an indefinite period of time, they had made a commitment to stay in touch and see where things led. "If I was free and there was not all this mayhem going on at the hotel, ah, lassie, I'd be on you faster than a speeding bullet."

She squeezed her eyes closed and shook her head gently. "Sorry to put a damper on our jolly outing."

He took her hand briefly. "You didna do that. Perhaps you can lend me your professional expertise. What's your take on the others?"

"Ah, let me see now." Helen stared ahead at the liquor bottles on the shelves behind the bar. "Anthony, a man of fine taste and acerbic wit … He could be our dastardly killer. Patrick's an odd duck—I think he's more likely. Charley comes off as all matey-matey, but there's something going on, and Yvette is obviously manipulated. I can see that ending in an abusive relationship. I hope I'm wrong."

"Wanda?"

"Wanda as in a serial killer? Hardly—although I'm no expert in psychopath profiling. She's emotionally fragile, but not insane."

"You think the murderer is insane?"

Helen assumed what Rex guessed was her professional look with students—an expression that suggested she was prepared to consider anything without prejudice. "I think the person is under severe stress," she said carefully.

"What makes you say that?"

"The behaviour seems erratic—first planned, then erratic, I mean."

"How do you know the first murder was planned?"

Helen offered him her crisps. "Sorry, I've been hogging these." He declined with a wave of his hand. "I heard you discussing the cyanide outside Charley's door," she told him. "I didn't catch much of what you were saying. I came upstairs for a ball of wool and slipped away before you saw me."

"You weren't alarmed?"

"At the time I thought it was a theoretical conversation, maybe to do with one of your cases."

"And the erratic behaviour ... What do you mean by that?"

"Well, the candlestick was carefully wiped clean of prints. But the way the BlackBerry and manuscript were got rid of point to hasty and possibly irrational acts."

"Aye, I considered that myself. What about the staff? Any suspicions?"

"An old lady, a cranky old man?" She laughed. "I'd be surprised, but when it really comes down to it, I can't imagine it being any of the people at the hotel."

"It has to be one of them. What about Rosie?"

"I'd say not, but then one of my students at school got in trouble with the law. Pauline's a good girl really, but she has problems at home."

"Mrs. Bellows?"

"Least of all. Salt of the earth type."

Rex sighed ponderously.

"I wasn't much help was I?" Helen said. "What about me? How do you know it wasn't me who killed Henry and Miriam?"

He looked into her unwavering blue eyes. "I had to eliminate a few people, but if you turn out to be the murderer, Helen, my last shred of hope for humanity will go up in smoke."

With a sharp intake of breath, Helen looked away, and then back at him. "So, why did you never get married?" she asked with a forced lightness.

"I was. I'm a widower."

"Oh, I missed that one, didn't I? And there I was going on about your feelings toward women. You must think me an utter fool." Her head tilted forward, hair falling across her face concealing her expression. "How did she die—if you don't mind my asking?"

"Breast cancer." The lump grew in his throat. It had been four years since he lost Fiona, but the pain and injustice of her death lurked beneath the surface, a rip tide ready to drag him under when he least expected it.

"Rex, how awful … Children?"

"A boy. Eighteen. I even have the requisite photo." He reached into his pocket for his wallet.

"Ready to settle up?" the barman asked.

"No hurry." Rex extracted a head and shoulders snapshot of his son taken during his last term at school. "This is Campbell."

"Handsome," Helen said, scrutinizing the picture in her hand, "though I don't see much of a resemblance."

"No, he got his blonde hair from his mother. And he's lanky, not stocky like meself."

"He looks very formal in his tie."

"Aye, he looks like it's choking him."

Helen laughed, and Rex was glad to see the tense mood between them broken. "So, is he a chip off the old block? Planning to go into law?"

"Noo. He's not really one for the books. He's studying marine science in Florida. He decided he wanted to save the dolphins."

"That's very commendable." Helen returned the photo.

"It would be, but I think it was more a question of sun, surfing, and scoping out girls in thongs. Anyway, he's staying with his roommate in Miami for Christmas." Rex drained the last of the Guinness and wiped off his mustache with a paper napkin.

The barman approached, drying a glass. "Are you staying at the hotel?"

"Aye. D'ye know anybody up there?"

"I'm acquainted with the cook, Sandy Bellows. She joins her husband of an evening for darts. A dab hand, she is." The barman, a middle-aged man with elaborate tattoos on his forearms, paused to think. "I don't know the new girl, but her sister used to come in all the time with her young man. He worked for the phone company—heard he moved to Essex. Marie went home to London in July last year to share her birthday with her sister, and we never saw her again. Killed on the seventh, the day of her birthday. Nobody'll forget that day in a hurry."

"Tragic," Helen said with feeling.

The barman eyed her with a glimmer of primal interest. Rex was stunned by the emotions that look roused in him—pride mixed with a protective instinct that made him want to grab the man by the throat. Rex, me old man, he thought with wry amusement.

"I wouldn't live in London for nothing," the bartender was telling Helen. "Nor in any big city. I like it right here where it's peaceful and nothing happens out of the ordinary, except for a freak snow storm." He winked at her. "One for the road?" he asked them.

"Not for me," Rex said. "Helen?" She shook her head. "But I'll buy a bottle of Croft Sherry off you if I may. For Clifford," he explained to Helen as the barman went to fetch one down from the shelf. "And a bottle of your best vintage port," he called after him.

A local who had appropriated the neighboring bar stool leaned in toward Rex. "There were two men from the hotel in here before the snow started," he imparted in a broad Sussex dialect. "Saying as how they'd like to give the old manor a face-lift, if they could get it for a knockdown price. I think one of them was in the antiques business."

"Anthony Smart," Helen murmured.

"Got quite boisterous after a few shots."

"I remember him and his young friend," the barman said, returning with the bottles. "Thought I'd have to throw 'em out." He rung up the total and Rex delved into his wallet.

"I don't suppose your phone is working?" Rex asked.

The man lifted the receiver of the phone behind the bar, put it to his ear, and shook his head.

Rex cursed to himself. He'd wanted to call home and ask the housekeeper if a letter had come for him postmarked Iraq. "Oh, I almost forgot." He pulled a sheet of paper from his coat pocket. "Could ye put this sign up somewhere? A puppy was abandoned by the station."

The barman nodded and took the sheet, wishing them a good Christmas.

As Rex and Helen headed toward the entrance, she whispered, "Did you feel me kick you when he was going on about nothing out of the ordinary ever happening in Swanmere? I couldn't keep my face straight."

A blast of frigid air hit Rex as he held the door open for her. "Well, time to head back," he said, collecting the skis and poles he had propped against the wall.

Helen pouted in jest. "Must we?"

"Aye, lass. I've undertaken an investigation in the absence of the police. No one can leave until they've been cleared."

"I hope nothing happened while we were gone," Helen said, sounding slightly out of breath as she bent over to tighten her bootlaces.

The movement stretched the fabric of her ski pants over her backside, and Rex thought it a pity he had nothing better to entertain himself with later than a dreary game of charades.

And the more daunting challenge of catching the killer.

ELEVEN

HELEN POINTED ACROSS THE street from the pub. "Oh, look, there's a shop open on the corner."

Rex resisted the impulse to look at his watch, though he was now anxious to get back to the hotel. "Do you need anything?"

"Not really, but I never pass up the opportunity to look. There might be something interesting in the way of souvenirs."

Rex carried the skis through the slush to the store. The front door opened with a tinkle.

A young Pakistani stood reading a paper behind the counter. "Most Merry Christmas," he greeted them. "And how may I be helping you today?"

Rex felt he should buy something to reward the man for being open on Christmas Eve and asked for his brand of tobacco while Helen surveyed the shelves.

"Oh, look at these," she squealed, holding out a pair of earrings in the shape of swans.

"These are very popular," the man enthused. "They are hand-crafted by my wife using sterling silver and turquoise stones for the eyes."

Rex indulgently held out his hand for the earrings and asked the shopkeeper to add them to his purchase.

"Oh, Rex, thank you. I love them!"

The man smiled happily as he packed the earrings in a small box wadded with cotton wool. They wished him a Happy Christmas and left the shop.

"Isn't it lucky we went in there?" Helen chirped as they retrieved their skis. "Now that nice man can tell his wife how much we liked her jewellery and that it was worth staying open today."

"Aye," Rex said, suppressing a grin. It never failed to amaze him how women always managed to find a way to justify their purchases.

———

It was almost dark by the time they finally made it back up the hill through the forest. His gloves had become soaked through when Helen, toppling into a shallow ravine, had dislodged her ski and he'd had to wipe off the ice to get her boot back in the binding. The lights blazing in the windows of the hotel were a welcome sight, and Rex hoped all was as peaceful inside as it looked from the south garden.

He stood his skis against the wall by the scullery door and helped Helen off with hers. Once inside, he gratefully pulled the boots off his feet.

Mrs. Smithings waylaid them in the kitchen. "Good afternoon, Ms. d'Arcy. What a nice colour you have in your cheeks."

"Oh, we had a wonderful time."

"I dare say you did," the hotel owner replied, watching with a curious expression as Helen walked on through the kitchen. She turned her attention to Rex. "Reginald, you never cease to amaze me—you found yet another way across the snow. Even as a child, you were always one step ahead of everyone else. How was the skiing?"

Rex coughed in apology. "I didn't want to disturb you earlier. I'll put everything back where I found it."

"You are quite welcome to use the skis. I would have offered them to you had I remembered we still had them."

"Thank you. Oh, by the way, are you missing a key?"

"Yes. Did you find it? Rosie misplaced hers when she was cleaning upstairs yesterday. I had to give her mine."

"I think I know where the other one is. How many master keys do you have?"

"Three. Mine, the one I give Louise—which is now in your possession—and Rosie's. I get them back at the end of the day and lock them up in the safe. I keep mine on my person."

Rex thanked her again for the use of the skis and proceeded on his way. Clifford sat at the pine table slicing the bottoms off Brussels sprouts. Rex decided to leave the sherry in his pocket until the old man was alone.

"What delicious recipe have you prepared for our tea?" he asked Mrs. Bellows, who was sharpening her carving knife with gusto at the counter, no doubt in readiness for the turkey the following day.

"Marzipan-covered fruit cake topped with royal icing."

Rex was not sure he liked the sound of that. Marzipan was almond paste and the thought of eating it made him anxious.

"I've been feeding the cake brandy since November," the cook added. "It's full of currants, raisins, and cherries, a bit like your Scottish Whisky Dundee."

"Aye, my mother makes that, but without the whisky."

Mrs. Bellows shook her head in disapproval. "Fancy that. I put in at least two tablespoons of brandy. And I add chopped walnuts, citron peel, and angelica to make it extra special."

"You have forty-five minutes until tea," Mrs. Smithings reminded him.

As Rex passed the drawing room, he caught sight of Helen chatting to Patrick and Anthony. Approaching the front door, he noticed shadows moving behind the frosted swirls of glass. Through a clear pane in the sidelight, he saw a bareheaded Charley and a hooded Yvette standing beside a snowman. While her husband studded the face with stones, forming a mirthless grin and sightless eyes, Yvette stuck twigs in its sides for arms. She was wearing smooth-soled fashion boots, and Rex hoped she wouldn't slip on the patches of ice glistening beneath the porch light.

He considered warning her to be careful and donating his scarf to the snowman, but the prospect of a nice warm bath lured him on up the stairs. Rosie was running a carpet sweeper along the landing. "Do you never get a rest, lass?" he asked.

She made a resigned face. "Mrs. Smithings promised me a bonus for all the extra work. I'm saving up for a car."

"What sort of car are you thinking of buying?"

"A Mini Cooper."

"Good choice. I have one of those."

"You do?" Rosie looked surprised. "I imagine you in a bigger car."

"I'm all about fuel efficiency. If I have to travel long distances, I go by train. That way I can get some work done."

"I'll never take the train again," Rosie declared.

"Oh, Rosie, I'm sorry. I heard about your sister and I forgot. How clumsy of me."

"It's all right," the girl said with an effort, and then in a more cheerful voice: "You're all bundled up. Did you go out somewhere?"

"Aye, down to the pub."

"That must have been fun."

"It was. I heard your sister used to go to the Swanmere Arms."

"They do like to gossip in the village, don't they?"

"So, what brought you here?"

"I thought there might be an opportunity for advancement. Marie talked about how lonely Mrs. Smithings was and how there were no young relatives to leave all this to." Rosie looked about her in some awe. "She said if she stayed long enough, Mrs. Smithings might leave her something. Mrs. Smithings still calls me Marie sometimes."

"Aye, she gets a little confused on occasion. Anyhow, I best get on with my bath or I'll miss tea."

"Wouldn't want to miss that," Rosie said.

Rex smiled and crossed to his room. As he put his hand on the knob, he remembered. "Ah, Rosie? Did you get your key back?" He imagined she gave a start.

"No."

He entered his room, pleased to see that the bed had been properly made and a new bar of lavender soap placed on a clean hand towel. Quickly exchanging his layers of clothes for his bathrobe, he grabbed his wash bag and scooted to the men's room while Rosie's back was turned, embarrassed to be seen in a state of undress.

The bathroom had been modernized back in the sixties. The copper pipes shuddered as water cascaded into the white tub, spewing steam from the faucet. Hot water really did have its own distinctive smell, Rex thought. It was reminiscent of something. He paused in the act of untying his flannel belt, recalling the precise moment he had made that discovery. He'd been no more than eleven, and it was here, in this house. He and Rodney were canoeing at the old mill, shooting down the short white-water rapids, the river glacial even in summer. Rodney upturned the canoe and they clambered, frozen-limbed and shivering, onto the bank and sought the remedy of a hot bath. And now Rodney Smithings was dead.

Easing into the scalding water, Rex guessed it must be a little past four. Splashing about in his haste, he soaped his washcloth and scrubbed from the back of his ears all the way to his toes, which were thawing out in almost excruciating pain. He swept the towel from the chair and briskly dried himself. The mirror was misted up. No matter: he would shave in his room.

The face that presented itself five minutes later was ruddy and smooth around his whiskers, which were graying to the ginger shade of sandstone. He hesitated over the blue sweater and decided on his camel-colored one instead. Surely Mrs. Smithings wouldn't object to that. Why did he care? Fear of being rebuked, no doubt dating back to his childhood, he guessed. Ludicrous that he should be afraid of her censure, even now.

With a last look around the room, he picked up the paper bag containing the sherry and made for the drawing room. Helen was seated on a sofa beside Patrick with her anorak and scarf spread around her, everyone intent on watching Anthony in the midst of a pantomime. The charades had begun, the gaiety and colored lights on the tree belying the presence of murder. Rex took a chair.

"We were just warming up while we waited for you and Wanda," Charley told him. "We haven't assigned teams yet. It's a free for all."

Anthony, his face animated above his gray V-neck sweater, laid two fingers on his arm.

"Film and book title, five words," Helen informed Rex. "This is the first word. It's two syllables."

Anthony mimed shooting himself in the head, then stabbing himself, and collapsed in a dramatic pose on the floor.

"Murder!" Charley and Patrick cried out in unison.

Rex stared at the entranced faces. How quickly people forgot.

Anthony touched his nose while pointing to Charley and then Patrick. Next he held up two fingers and made a sign as though measuring a tiny fish.

"Preposition!" Helen exclaimed.

Anthony made the pointing gesture again.

"You can't shout out unless it's the actual word," Yvette objected.

"What's a preposition again?" Patrick asked.

Anthony sighed eloquently.

"It's a part of speech," Helen replied. "Above, under, over, on—"

Anthony pointed.

"Murder on something something something," Helen reflected aloud.

"Anthony, you can't do that," Yvette complained. "Helen was just explaining to Patrick what a prep-thing was. She wasn't actually guessing."

Yvette does whine a lot, Rex thought.

"I was just trying to move things along."

Charley jumped up in excitement. "Wait, I've got it! Murder on the Oriental Express!"

"*Orient* Express, not Oriental," Patrick piped up. "Murder on the Orient Express."

Anthony pointed at his nose and Patrick simultaneously, and everyone clapped except Charley.

"Not fair!" he exclaimed at Patrick. "You mightn't have guessed it if I hadn't been so close. But well done, mate," he added graciously.

"Let's do another one," Anthony said. "Your turn, Patrick."

The young man stood up and took Anthony's place on the center of the rug. After a brief pause, he pretended to crank an old-fashioned movie camera.

Rex studied each participant in turn. What did he know about these people? Patrick was twenty-eight and a graduate of the Slade School of Art. He'd joined Smart Design as a faux and mural artist four years ago. Anthony, a decade older, also owned a half share in an antiques shop in Kensington specializing in timepieces from the Georgian, Regency, and Victorian periods—as Rex had memorized from a conversation with him.

His knowledge of the Perkinses was even more sketchy. Yvette, twenty-one, worked as a receptionist at a solicitors' firm in Wok-ing. She and Charley, twenty-six, had met at a Rave concert. Helen, forty-four, had brought her newly divorced friend Wanda to Swanmere for a change of scene: "somewhere peaceful where she could re-center herself."

Rosie brought in the tray at that moment, disrupting his thoughts along with the game of charades.

"We'll have to continue after tea," Yvette declared.

I hope not, Rex said to himself, thinking of a viable excuse to leave straight after his tea. Ah, yes, the wee dog. He hadn't seen it since this morning.

"I admit *Murder on the Orient Express* wasn't in the best possible taste," Anthony said. "But it's the first thing that came to mind."

Rosie glanced round at the guests in surprise from where she was setting out the plates.

"Is that the mystery where everyone dies one by one?" Helen inquired.

"No, you're thinking of *And Then There Were None*," Anthony said. "In *Murder on the Orient Express,* everyone is involved in the murder of one passenger."

Helen rose from the sofa. "Well, I had better get Wanda. Has anyone seen her?"

"Not today," Charley replied.

Everyone else looked blank.

"You should join in the charades, Rex," Yvette said, on her way to the tea table. "You look so serious sitting there by yourself."

He smiled distantly, wondering who among them might be involved in a real-life charade—acting out their role as an innocent bystander and succeeding in duping everyone around them. It would take a person of nerve, of *sang-froid*. He had complimented Charley for possessing just such a quality. Who else fit the bill?

"Mind if I take a look at your sketches?" he asked Patrick, indicating the pad on the sofa. Perhaps the drawings would reveal something his naked eye could not.

"Help yourself."

While the others crowded around the Victorian table, Rex flipped through the pad, which showed numerous studies in charcoal of Anthony's face from various angles. Patrick had managed to capture his slightly sardonic expression. He had done some caricature portraits of the other residents as well. Henry Lawdry looked a bit lecherous, Rosie sly, and Mrs. Smithings demented. Rex chuckled to himself.

"These are excellent," he told Patrick. "I particularly like this one of Clifford." The furtive figure in cap and tweeds—attire befitting a fly-fisherman after salmon in Scotland, though in its current state more suited to a scarecrow—was captioned "Faithful Family Retainer."

Turning the page, Rex came to the picture of the robin, the breast delicately colored in red. Another watercolor showed a portion of the room with Anthony in his armchair, Helen and Wanda on the sofa, and behind them, the round table and Christmas tree with its bells and burgundy bows. His eye focused on the table. He compared it to the actual table. "Rosie," he asked as the girl was leaving the room. "There's no coffeepot today."

"I thought the American lady was the only one who took coffee in the afternoon," she replied. "Will you be requiring some?"

"No, I never touch the stuff. I just wondered, that's all."

Rosie threw him a puzzled look as she stepped out the French doors into the hall.

"Coffee is probably not the best thing for someone with your condition," Anthony approved, returning to the fireplace with his tea. "I only drink it in small doses myself, and then only the Arabica beans which have half the caffeine of the other main variety."

Charley and Yvette sat down on the sofa with their tea and cake. "Anthony, you are a mine of useless information," the husband pointed out.

At that moment, Helen stumbled into the room.

"What's wrong, luv? You look pale as a ghost."

"W-Wanda." Helen delivered the word through frozen lips.

Rex leaped up from his armchair. "What do you mean?"

"She's … Oh, please, no! She's dead!"

Charley jumped up too, sloshing tea on the carpet. "Where is she?"

"In her room. She never got up this morning. I think she took an overdose. She's not breathing. I thought she was sleeping, but there's no pulse!" Helen burst into tears.

Rex was unsure whether to stay and console her or follow Charley up the stairs. He thrust the bottle of sherry into Anthony's hands. "Here, give Helen some of this," he directed, and ran after Charley.

He reached Wanda's door just as Charley was approaching the bed.

"She's getting stiff," Charley said. "She's been dead at least six hours."

That would put her death at around the time he and Helen left for the village, Rex calculated. She had said Wanda was sleeping late.

Charley straightened up from examining the body. "I'll get a thermometer and record time and temperature for the police."

"Overdose?"

"I don't think so. There are no pill containers by the bedside and no suicide note, which you'd expect if someone tried to kill themselves. Wanda would have written one of those, I'm sure. She'd want everyone to know why she did it. And see this? The pillow beside her is scrunched up. I think someone used it to suffocate her."

Rex took in Wanda's perfectly manicured nails, the glossy ringlets spread on the pillow. "There's no sign of a struggle. Her nightdress isn't even askew. She must have been asleep or else not been surprised to see the person in the room." It would have had to be someone strong, he reasoned. Though petite, Wanda was in good shape.

"My guess is she was smothered by that pillow, just like Desdemona. Except there's no Othello or any equivalent of a jealous husband that I'm aware of."

"So, you know your Shakespeare, Charley?"

"Amateur dramatics."

"Really."

"Why d'you say it like that?"

"Look, we're up against the clock so I'm just going to dispense with etiquette and ask you outright about an exchange I heard between you and Yvette in your room this morning. Something about murder, and Henry, and getting found out, and I don't know what else without referring to my notes."

"Oh, that." Charley scratched his lightly stubbled chin. "Well, it's like this. Yvette stopped taking the pill without telling me. When I found out, I went ballistic. I wanted her to have an abortion—I mean, we don't have the dough for our own place, and living at her mum's with a baby, well, it would be the *end*. Anyway, Yvette said that was murder and she's right. I've had time to think about it and I've done a complete three-sixty—I want us to have the little blighter."

He opened his arms wide. "I just don't know how we're going to be able to afford a deposit on a flat. I got into a bit of trouble gambling and owe some money. Anyhow, Yvette got all upset about my first reaction and accused me of fancying Rosie and I told her she was one to talk after flirting with old Henry and, well...," Charley tapered off. "Does that answer your question?"

"Aye, you always seem to have an answer for everything." Or maybe Charley was a good improviser.

"We Cockneys are known for thinking on our feet," Charley said brightly. "We walk the walk and talk the talk. So, are we going to put Wanda into cold storage with Henry?"

"I think we'd better leave her here with the window open as the doctor instructed for the first body."

"Blimey. First a poisoning, then a clobbering, and now a smothering. I think I'll keep Yvette locked in our suite."

"Not a bad idea. It's been one murder a day since the first." Rex opened the bedside drawer and rummaged among the various items. The master key was missing.

"Here, check this out," Charley said, turning a page of the small photo album Rex had inventoried the night before. "It's a diary, and you are mentioned, mate—in very flattering terms, I might add."

"I thought it was just photos."

"Well, I never," Charley continued, immersed in the diary. "Talk about immature."

Rex reached for it, hoping to find something useful as he leafed through the pages written in a spiked longhand. The bulk of Wanda's recent entries was dedicated to her thoughts and feelings regarding her divorce, her New Year resolutions, and hyperbolic descriptions of the glorious snow, which turned to invective as the pages progressed: "*Sod this snow!*; *When's this bloody snow going to end?*"

He read the entry for yesterday, December 23: "*... Rosie left her key in my door this morning when she came in to clean. I took it and later went into Henry's room but couldn't find the antique cameo he promised me. No wonder—Anthony told me tonight he'd advised Y. to put it in the safe. How did the little minx get hold of it? I bet she stole it...*"

The next entry, for the same day but in different ink, must have been written late last night: "*Patrick curled my hair. New look for the New Year!! We argued about who had murdered Miriam. He thinks it's Clifford, though Rex doesn't appear to agree—he seems quite friendly with the old man. He had better hurry up and find the killer...*"

Amen to that, Rex thought, and read on:

"*Helen seems cosy with Rex, though she refuses to discuss it. I got a kiss off him under the mistletoe. I think he's rather hunky. He has*" *gorgeous green eyes that give off sparks when he is amused. I wonder what he's like in bed?!! ... "*

Rex felt his face go scarlet. *"... The other day, I saw Mrs. S. go into the safe behind the painting in the library. I was surprised to find it was an old-fashioned key lock safe—I suppose a combination safe is too high-tech for the old dragon. No cameo in there, but I came across something else of interest. I wonder if Rosie knows yet and if she told Charley. I think there is something going on between them. I caught them flirting yesterday in the library when Y. was playing Tiddlywinks with Henry. She's been looking very guilty since then ... "*

Overactive imagination or boredom, or both? Rex pocketed the diary. "You're in here too," he told Charley. "Featured with Rosie."

"Oh, that," Charley replied in an off-hand manner.

"Did you find anything else of interest lying around?"

"Nothing in the bathroom that she could have taken if she'd wanted to kill herself. I found this note from Helen by the door."

Rex read the folded sheet of hotel stationery.

Wanda,
Am skiing down to the village with Rex. Didn't want
to wake you. See you later.
Helen

As the men left the room, Helen came rushing up the stairs and bowled into Rex's arms. "I shouldn't have left her!" she wailed. "I was just so thrilled at the prospect of going down to the village."

"We can't be sure exactly what time it happened, hen."

"And there I was sitting in the pub telling you how emotionally fragile she was!" Helen sobbed against his chest.

"We don't think it was suicide," he said, cupping the back of her head in his hand.

Charley paused at the top of the stairs. "I'll go and tell the others, shall I?"

"Aye. Tell them to be on their guard. And let's try to keep everyone in one room for now." He turned his attention back to the woman in his arms. "Helen, listen to me. Did Wanda keep her door locked?"

Helen nodded. "I entered her room through mine when I found her and left through her door to the corridor. I should have gone in to check on her this morning, but I didn't want to wake her. I just slipped the note under the door to let her know I was going to the village."

"Shhh." He stroked her hair, which gave off an effervescent scent of lacquer. "Did you know Wanda had a spare key to Henry's room?"

Helen glanced up with a puzzled frown. "No, I didn't." She pulled away from him. "Do you think she could have taken it from Mrs. Smithings' office?"

"No, she stole it from Rosie. Mrs. Smithings keeps the keys locked up. The strange thing is, I couldna find the key just now when I searched the room, and Rosie told me she didn't have it either. It was there last night."

"I don't know anything about it."

"Wanda used the key to go into Lawdry's room and burn incense."

Helen furrowed her brow. "How bizarre. Maybe she was trying to transfer the grief over her divorce onto something she was more familiar with, like death. Her parents passed away last year."

"Did you see her after she left with Patrick last night?"

She shook her head. "I heard their voices next door, but then I fell asleep. I don't know how long Patrick was in there doing her hair."

"I'll ask Mrs. Smithings about the key, see if it found its way back to her."

Rex wondered how the proprietor was taking the news of a third death in her hotel.

TWELVE

CLIFFORD SAT AT THE old pine table working on the Brussels sprouts when Rex left Helen and came downstairs.

"Goodness, man. How many of those do you have left to do?" Rex asked.

"We'll be lucky if he's finished by Christmas morning," Mrs. Bellows remarked from the sink. "I'll have to do the peas and carrots myself."

"Clifford, I bought you a bottle of sherry. It's in the drawing room. Helen had a drop because she had a bit of a turn, but the rest is for you."

The old man's beady eyes lit up.

"Is she all right now?" the cook asked. "What happened?"

Apparently, she hadn't heard about Wanda. "She will be. By the way, it seems you're famous at the Swanmere Arms."

"'Bull's-Eye Bellows,' they call me in the village. Our team took the East Sussex darts trophy again this year."

"Well done. Anyway," Rex said turning back to Clifford. "The sherry is my way of saying thank you for looking after the wee dog. How is he, by the way? I brought him a treat."

"I keep him in the lodge now. He's right at home. Won't bother her there."

"He's getting fat off all the scraps from the kitchen," Mrs. Bellows added. "It's better than throwing stuff away."

"I put a sign up in the village with the hotel number on it. If they ever get the phones working, someone may call to claim him."

"Nar!" Clifford cried, staring accusingly at Rex. "Ee be mine now. 'Ee likes it 'ere. In the spring 'ee'll be chasing rabbits and 'aving 'isself a rare ould time."

Rex hesitated. "Well, I see no reason why you canna keep him. He was clearly abandoned. If Mrs. Smithings gives you trouble over it, I'll talk to her." Clifford looked appeased. "You could train him to go after the rats in the attic—terriers are hunting dogs. Have you got a name for him yet?"

"Rex."

"A grand name! And I'm glad he found a home. I hope I'll see him before I leave."

"I'll bring young Rex over later when She retires for the evenin' so you can see how well 'ee's doing."

"Well, give him this in the meantime." Rex deposited a sliver of moist cake on the table, and Clifford snatched it up and dropped it in his pocket with a speed Rex hadn't known the old man possessed. "Is Mrs. Smithings aboot?" he asked the cook.

"She's in the library looking over the accounts. There's more room at that desk. She said she didn't want to be disturbed for half an hour."

Returning to the deserted drawing room, Rex sank into an armchair and filled his pipe with slow deliberation. His gaze drifted across the navy blue and cream tones of the carpet and up the blue walls to the cross-beamed ceiling. A third murder to unravel. With a sigh of discouragement, he stuck the pipe in his mouth and wrote up his notes:

Patrick last-known person to see Wanda alive.
Rosie mentioned in diary flirting with Charley and in context of there being something in the safe that might interest her.
Key missing from Wanda's drawer.
People with access to room:
Patrick could have taken key when he was in Wanda's room styling her hair.
Rosie had Mrs. Smithings' key.

Pencil poised on the next line, Rex hesitated. Helen said the adjoining door to Wanda's room had been unlocked. This possibility was not one Rex wished to pursue, but he must explore every angle and not let his feelings for Helen blind him to the facts. He duly wrote:

Helen did not need key to enter Wanda's room.

Now he had to consider how Wanda's murder fitted in with the other two. Who had motive? Was it someone who wanted to discredit the hotel, hoping subsequently to purchase it at below market value? Or was it someone who wished to cause embarrassment to Mrs. Smithings? Perhaps the culprit harbored an old grievance against one of the guests and caused the multiple deaths as a cover-up. Or maybe it was a medical professional with a God complex who thought they could simply get away with murder.

If time would just stand still for a while, perhaps he could puzzle it all out clearly and calmly ... Time standing still, no ticking clock. Losing all sense of time in this place. No newspapers delivered in days. A stack of old ones by the hearth, ready for tinder. A burning manuscript. Charred bits of words. *1 Qa* ...

Rex sprang from his chair and rummaged through the pile of newspapers by the fireplace, skimming the headlines. *Al Qaeda.* Of course. The terrorist organization was all over the news. The "l" wasn't the number "one" but the letter "l"; "Qaeda" hadn't made it into the hotel library's old edition of the *Concise Oxford Dictionary.*

Where did that lead him in his investigations? Anthony's comment at breakfast about President Bush could implicate him as the arsonist. But did he murder the literary agent? On impulse, Rex retrieved his cell phone from his pocket and speed-dialed his mother's temporary number in Perth, surprised when the call held and his mother answered, "The McTaggart residence."

"Mother!"

"Reginald, is that you, dear? You sound so far away. Are ye well?"

"Aye, and yerself? How is Jean doing?"

"Better, I think. She ate some broth and kept it down. But I don't want ye running up those long distance cell phone minutes! Ye know how expensive those bills can be."

"Don't worry about that. I may not have long—my connection might be interrupted again."

"How is Dahlia, poor lamb?"

Rex could think of various ways to describe Mrs. Smithings. A lamb was not one of them. He decided not to go into details. "Bearing up fine," he told her.

"Have ye heard from Moira?"

Moira and his mother shared the same first name, which was why he referred to his girlfriend as Mrs. Wilcox, to avoid confusion. A member of the Charitable Ladies of Morningside like his mother, she had left Edinburgh's wealthy south-west district to restore schools and water purification systems in Baghdad.

"Not even a Christmas card," he said, closing the drawing room doors for privacy. "Mother, is Mrs. Smithings prone to violence?"

"No-oo! Why d'you say that? What's going on down there? Why are ye—"

"Mother!" Rex shouted into the phone—but the call had been dropped. He tried dialing again without success; his mother wouldn't call on her friend's phone, worried as she would be about cost. In any case, his line of inquiry was a long shot. Mrs. Smithings had not been around at the time of the first two murders and lacked the strength to commit the third. He wandered to the round table, which Rosie had not yet cleared, and served himself a cup of lukewarm tea.

Of everyone, Rosie had had the most opportunity to poison Lawdry, but no one recalled her serving him. The guests had all helped themselves. Could she have pushed Miriam down the stairs? According to Helen, she had been collecting teacups in this room. In any case, what motive did the young girl have for murdering the guests, especially if she had a stake in the hotel's success? Her sister had been hoping for something in Mrs. Smithings' will. Quite possibly Rosie was hoping for the same.

He was going round in circles and getting nowhere.

By the time he managed to make a few local calls, Mrs. Smithings had vacated the library, and he knocked at the parlor-office door. Her voice bade him come in.

"Hello, Reginald," she said from her desk. "No doubt you have come to talk about Wanda Martyr. Quite an extraordinary turn of events."

"Ah, you heard."

"Well, naturally. Walls have ears. Rosie told me. But we are going to keep it from Clifford and Mrs. Bellows if we can. We cannot afford to lose our cook. We're short-handed as it is."

Rex perched on a straight-back chair. "They'll find out soon enough. The police will be here asking questions. I was able to make a few calls on my mobile just now."

"When do you suppose they will arrive?"

"Tomorrow morning. And the village constable expects train service to resume the day after."

"I see. And whom will you put forward as your likely suspects?"

"At this point in time, everyone is a suspect and no one is a suspect."

"Poppycock. I'm sure you have formed an idea."

"Ideas are not facts. Actually, I wanted to ask you if you saw anyone go into Wanda Martyr's room this morning?"

"I was here in the parlour from eight until eleven, catching up on paper work and practicing on the pianoforte."

Rex noticed the instrument squashed in a corner. "Were all the rooms made up this morning?"

"I believe so." Mrs. Smithings sounded weary.

"I can imagine how exhausting this must be for you …"

"Can you? I wonder …" She reviewed her claw-like hands. "The arthritis alone causes chronic fatigue, you know. My playing is not what it used to be, but it helps to keep the fingers exercised."

"Aye, I noticed you had rheumatoid arthritis medication in your suite."

"The anti-inflammatory pills work better on the smaller joints. My elbows and shoulders suffer most."

"Clifford has the same complaint," Rex remarked, nodding in a gesture of sympathy.

"And complains about it incessantly!"

Rex listened patiently to her ailments, though Mrs. Smithings was no older than his mother, a woman still spry for her age. They'd both had their sons late in life.

Rex picked up a small oval-framed photograph of Rodney taken at about the age Rex had seen him on his last visit to Swanmere. "I'm sorry about what happened to your son. I spoke briefly with my mother this evening before we were cut off. She sends her warmest regards."

"Dear Moira." Mrs. Smithings took the photograph and gazed at it through her reading spectacles. "It was too big a sacrifice, Reginald. He was all I had left."

All those sons lost in Iraq and Afghanistan, all those grieving mothers. Rex considered how his own mother would cope if something happened to him. The thought made his heart contract most painfully.

Mrs. Smithings returned the photograph to its place on the table. With nothing else to add, Rex retreated to the drawing room where the fire flickered cheerfully in welcome counterpoint to the formal atmosphere of the parlor. He was itching to look in the library safe and see what Wanda had referred to in her diary, but decided to wait until he was sure he wouldn't be seen. Settling into an armchair, he pulled out his notebook.

When Rosie entered the room to announce dinner an hour later, he was so absorbed by the lists and Venn diagrams covering the pages that he jumped in his seat.

"Where are the others?" she asked in surprise.

"Keeping to their rooms, I expect. I'll round them up for you."

"I'd be so grateful. My legs are killing me. I've been up and down those stairs like a yo-yo."

"Rosie," he said. "Did you make up room number five this morning—Ms. Martyr's room?"

"I knocked, and when she didn't answer, I went in. But she was asleep so I crept out again."

"What time was this?"

"Must've been about eleven."

"Are you sure?" Wanda would probably have been dead by then.

"Yes. I left her room until last since she sometimes slept late. She was out like a light."

"Whose key did you use?"

"I didn't need a key. The door from Ms. d'Arcy's room was unlocked. I did her room first." Rosie chewed her bottom lip.

"What is it, lass?"

144

"Well, about an hour before that, I was about to knock on Ms. d'Arcy's door to deliver clean towels when I heard her say something like, 'Oh, Wanda, I'm sorry to have to do this but you deserve it. You took Paul from me and I'm not going to let you stand in my way again.' The door was slightly ajar and I heard her clearly. I didn't think much about it at the time, but later, when I learned that her friend had died, I—I …"

"You interpreted the words in a different light."

"Exactly."

"What did Wanda say in reply?"

"Nothing. It was like Ms. d'Arcy was talking to herself, only she sounded a bit worked up. Anyway, I had my hand to the door, ready to knock, and decided not to as it sounded private."

Rex nodded and turned toward the French doors. What was the significance of what Rosie had heard Helen say? The fact that Rosie mentioned the name Paul gave her story a ring of truth. Deep in thought, he mounted the stairs and knocked at the honeymoon suite, then Helen's room, and finally at Patrick and Anthony's. "Dinner is ready," he told the guests. He escorted Helen downstairs. "Feeling better?" he asked.

She nodded shakily. "A bit. I wrote a letter to Paul explaining what happened—as far as I could explain. It's easier than talking on the phone. I haven't really spoken to him since he ditched me for Wanda all those years ago. I'm sure he'll be glad he won't have to pay alimony now," she said with a trace of bitterness.

By the time they reached the dining room, a starter of smoked salmon adorned with a round of lemon awaited on each of the six plates. Anthony and Patrick followed them into the room.

"Well, isn't this cosy?" Anthony commented in ironic fashion, taking his seat at the head of the table between Rex and Patrick.

Yvette and Charley completed the group.

"Just us three couples left," the Cockney said, shaking out his linen napkin, which had been folded into a swan.

Yvette admired hers. "How sweet." She continued to stare at it, her mind clearly elsewhere.

"Aye. Helen was telling me this afternoon how swans mate for life."

"A bit like you and Charley," Anthony told Yvette waspishly. "You two are inseparable. Every time a crime is committed in this house, you always seem to be conveniently together—and absent."

"What's that supposed to mean?"

"It means you can never be accounted for."

"We were outside building a snowman this afternoon. Apart from that we were with other people."

"Look, we're all a bit rattled," Patrick jumped in. "None of us is above suspicion."

An uncomfortable silence spread across the table.

Clifford brought the dog into the room, creating a welcome diversion. "Young Rex 'ere to see you," he announced. "Eh taught 'im to raise 'is paw." Lowering his back in a series of jerks, the old man added a log to the fire.

"Here boy!" Charley called, holding out a piece of salmon.

"This will go down in the annals as one of the most surreal Christmases I ever spent," Anthony remarked.

"And to think I could have gone to Aviemore," Helen said. "Then Wanda would never have come here and she'd still be alive."

146

Rex reached out his hand to comfort her.

"D'you think Clifford knows about the murders?" Patrick asked Rex when the old man left. "He's pretty deaf, isn't he? Probably doesn't catch much."

"Mrs. Smithings wanted to keep it from the staff."

"Ha!" Anthony replied with derision. "She acts as though nothing's amiss. She was tinkling away on her pianoforte all morning. A bit like Nero sawing on his fiddle while Rome burned, if you ask me."

Patrick pronged the lemon with his fork. "It's creepy, that's all. Three murders, all by different methods. Who's next?"

"There's something you're not telling us about how Lawdry died, isn't there?" Anthony asked Rex.

"I didn't want to alarm you."

"Alarm us! You must be joking."

"We couldn't be more alarmed," Patrick explained. "We just want the truth. I mean, it might be safer for us if we left."

"You and Helen made it as far as the village today," Yvette added, addressing Rex.

"We skied," Helen replied. "And anyway it's dark now." She had barely touched her food, Rex noticed. "Besides, none of us can leave until the police get here. They'll want to question everyone."

"There may not be any of us left by then," Anthony objected. "Why should we stick around?"

Rex really had no answer to that. "Look. I think I may know what's going on, but there are pieces that don't fit into the puzzle. If I'm right, there won't be any more murders as long as nobody meddles. I think that's what happened to Wanda."

"Wanda was murdered because she tried to solve the case?" Patrick asked.

"It was more a case of her stumbling onto something."

"What?"

"I can't tell you that for now. But once I have all the pieces, I will, I promise."

"In the meantime, can you tell us who you think did it?" Anthony insisted. "At least tell us if it's one of us or not."

"I have what I term 'valid assumptions,' mostly arrived at by the process of elimination, but I need proof."

"Doesn't sound all that reassuring to me. What do you have to say for yourself, Charley? You're not usually so quiet."

"Well, apart from this whole thing putting a kybosh on my honeymoon, I'm just as stressed as the next person. But I think we should trust Rex's judgment."

"Me too," Helen said, and Rex inwardly thanked them for their loyalty.

After dinner, when the other guests were occupied in the drawing room, Rex retired to the library. Two oil paintings hung in the room: a landscape of a mill, after the Constable school, and the bowl of mellow fruit he'd contemplated the previous afternoon while waiting to ask Yvette about the cameo. Wanda had been looking for the brooch when she opened the safe. She'd spied on Mrs. Smithings standing by one of the paintings. Rex deplored the owner's lack of foresight. Anyone with a master key had access to the safe if they knew where it was located.

Wanda must have been at the door when she saw the owner, in which case the safe had to be behind the still life, since the other picture was on the opposite wall and not visible from the door. He closed it behind him and crossed to the built-in bookshelf. The painting would not lift off the wall. Nor was there enough space among the shelves for it to slide in any direction. He felt around the frame for a hinge. If Mrs. Smithings had not seen Wanda, the painting must swing out to the left—like so. He inserted the key in the iron safe hidden behind it and opened the door.

Inside he found a master key, an assortment of stationery, and a locked jewelry box. Mrs. Smithings presumably kept the key to that somewhere else—not that someone couldn't just run off with the box. Another dreadful oversight. She must be getting senile.

Sorting through folders containing various deeds, he came across a business-size, creamy white envelope in which was folded the owner's will dated three months ago. He scanned the pages and saw that Mrs. Smithings was leaving Swanmere estate, lock, stock and barrel, to Rosie Porter, along with small bequeaths to various staff, and her pearls to his mother. Rex locked the safe and put the painting back in its place.

A rap sounded at the library door.

"Come in!" he called.

Helen appeared. "I hope I'm not disturbing you."

"It's all right, lassie. Did you need anything?"

"It's just that I … I can't sleep with Wanda lying dead in the next room," she said in a rush, a shimmer of tears in her eyes. "Can I stay in your room? I wouldn't feel safe anywhere else. No hanky-panky, I promise."

He acquiesced with a gentle nod and put an arm around her shoulders. Her tears seemed real enough. "Wanda must have meant a great deal to you."

"I feel bad because when I left her the note this morning I was having petty thoughts about how I wasn't going to let her spoil my outing with you. I was glad she was sleeping late so I didn't have to include her in my plans."

"It's the grief that's making you feel overly guilty."

"You're right, and that's what I'd be telling someone if the roles were reversed, only it's not easy to be rational when it's you in the middle of it."

"I know. When Fiona died I blamed myself for all the flowers I should have bought her."

Helen sighed tremulously. "What a bloody awful Christmas."

"Where are the others?"

"In the drawing room. It's like we're all scared to leave. I had Charley escort me here. You trust Charley, don't you?"

Rex hesitated. He didn't like what he'd just found out. He recalled Wanda hinting in her diary at something going on between Rosie and Charley. Rosie was an alluring young woman who'd been left a sizeable inheritance. Charley was faced with gambling debts and the prospect of living at his in-laws with a baby he'd not planned for. Had Rosie told him about her good fortune? Did she even know?

"I'd like to think you're safe with him," Rex hedged. Helen was standing so close he could feel her warmth. Her face lifted toward his in slow motion. He blinked and turned away, clearing his throat. "I'll take you upstairs," he said. "I'm finished here."

When they reached the upper landing, he went to his room while Helen cleared out her belongings from her suite. He took his wash bag to the men's room, leaving his door on the latch. In passing, he tried Lawdry's door and found it locked. No need to remind everyone to keep their doors locked, judging by the mood at dinner.

Rex fervently prayed he was right about his valid assumptions.

THIRTEEN

"Can we keep a small light on?" Helen asked from the bed as Rex prepared to join her in pajamas buttoned all the way to his throat. "It'll make me feel safer."

She snuggled up to him in her flannel nightdress, and Rex took her in his arms to comfort her. The contact caused an uncontrollable reaction. He tried to focus instead on the Presbyterian bible by his bedside. Perhaps this was the purpose of his mother's first commandment: *Keep a bible by yer bedside!* He never would have credited her with such foresight. Unfortunately, his body did not seem to want to follow his pure thoughts.

"Hen, I'm going to have to turn my back or we'll both regret it in the morning."

"You may regret it, but I won't," Helen sniffled. "At least I know I don't turn you off."

"No, and I have a roaring election to prove it."

Helen giggled. "Is that rhyming slang?"

"Aye, I got it off Charley."

"Just think what I could do if I touched you." She put her small hand on his shoulder blade. "You are such a bear of a man, so cuddly." She rubbed her feet on his heels.

"Stop it, lass, stop it right there."

"I'm just warming my feet. They feel like icicles."

"What would Square Root say if he knew you were in bed with a Scotsman?"

"I'm so far from thinking about Clive. You have completely distracted me with your misplaced gallantry."

"Helen…"

"Yes?"

"Do you smell smoke?"

"From the chimney?"

"The fire's not lit." Rex leaped out of bed and dashed into the corridor.

Wreaths of smoke escaped from under Henry Lawdry's door. Rex ran back to his room and retrieved the master key from his trouser pocket.

"What's wrong?" Helen asked from the pillows.

"There's a fire in the next room. Get dressed and raise the alarm." He ran out again and burst into Lawdry's room.

The bed was alight. Rex grabbed a pitcher off the chest of drawers and filled it from the sink. As he approached the bed, his bare feet encountered sodden carpet. He had no time to wonder what he was stepping on, but he didn't smell gasoline—his first thought. Dousing the flames, he brought the fire under control. He then flung open the wardrobe, pulled down the spare blankets, and piled them on top of the bed, smothering the rest of the flames.

When he switched on the main light, he saw that Mr. Lawdry's face had escaped the ravages of fire, presumably because his head rested on a flame-resistant pillow, Rex realized when he examined it. Between the corpse's shoulder and pillow, he discovered a half-burned box of matches with the picture of the hotel curled and blackened at the edges. A red smudge caught his attention.

Within minutes, voices and footsteps converged in the corridor. He turned to see Patrick and Anthony standing in the doorway in their dressing gowns, Charley behind them in pajamas and bare feet. Next, he heard urgent female voices, Helen's and Yvette's. "It's all right," he told them all. "The fire's out. I got to it in time."

"Did poor old Henry get cremated?" Charley asked.

"Not too badly, but I suspect someone wanted the body destroyed and all evidence of cyanide poisoning along with it. I can't imagine any other reason why someone would have wanted to burn the old man."

"So that's how he died," Anthony said. "You never told us it was cyanide."

"That's what we think, based on what was found."

"Dear old Henry," Yvette said, clutching Charley's arm. "He didn't deserve any of this."

"Did you wake the staff?" Rex asked Helen who huddled beneath a cashmere shawl thrown over her nightgown.

Her teeth chattered. "No, I was too scared to go to the staff quarters. It's dark on that side of the house."

"Well, no need to now. The danger has passed. I'll have a word with Mrs. Smithings in the morning."

"I hope she has some smelling salts handy," Anthony remarked.

"She seems to be bearing up quite well, considering everything that's happened," Helen said.

"Aye. She always was an old battle-axe."

"I'm going back to our room," Helen said. "It's freezing out here."

Charley raised an eyebrow. "*Our* room?"

Rex ignored him. Standing on his tiptoes, he reached up and unscrewed the smoke detector above the door. As he suspected, the battery had been removed. Anyone under six feet would have needed a chair to reach the alarm. Patrick, the next tallest after him, was no more than five-eleven. Rex looked about the room and found a few items of furniture that could have served the purpose, but nothing retained a visible footprint.

By the time he finished his investigation, all but Charley had dispersed to their rooms.

"Fancy a dram of choice port downstairs?" Rex asked him.

"Don't mind if I do. I'll see to Yvette first and meet you out here."

When Rex returned to his room, Helen was waiting for him on the bed.

"Anything new?" she asked.

"I do know there's a devious mind at work." He buckled his corduroys over his pajama bottoms and flung his arms into a sweater.

"Aren't you coming back to bed?"

"Nay, lass. I have a theory I need to work on." Locating his sheepskin moccasins, he slid his frozen feet into them.

"That's too bad. I wanted to work on breaking down your resistance."

A mischievous look brightened her eyes. The thought of her rubbing her feet against his calves sent erotic visions to his brain. If Charley had not been waiting for him, the temptation of cuddling with Helen in a warm bed might have proved irresistible.

"I'll bring you up a cup of tea in the morning," he told her.

"Tea? As in, would you like to come in for a cup of coffee?"

"Tea as in tea, you shameless hussy. Now, lock the door when I leave."

"What good will that do if someone has Wanda's master key? These doors don't have bolts."

"Aye, security is downright lax around here."

He showed Helen how to prop a chair under the door handle. "Call me on my mobile if you need to," he said, retrieving one of his business cards from his briefcase and handing it to her. "I can be upstairs in less than two minutes. Now, see me out and get to bed. You're shivering."

He grabbed the bottle of port, along with the toothbrush glass and left the room. The door lock clicked behind him and wood thumped on wood as the chair was slotted into position. *Good lass.*

Charley loitered at the top of the stairs.

"Is Yvette safely tucked in for the rest of the night?" Rex asked.

"She was pissed I wasn't staying, but how could anyone sleep with all this going on?"

They made their way downstairs to the drawing room where Charley stoked the dying embers. Rex would have liked to close the French doors to keep out the draft, but he wanted to be able to look out into the hall. As he dropped into a well-worn armchair, the seat cushion sounded like a bagpipe tuning up, while the compressed springs beneath reverberated in groaning protest. "Time for some new chairs," he remarked.

"And a new sofa. This one's probably stuffed full of horsehair. Some honeymoon. I'll throttle Yvette's mum when I see her. 'A nice romantic place in the country with good home-cooked food,'" he mimicked. "A deathtrap, more like."

"Something to tell your grandbairns about."

When Charley didn't answer, Rex looked over at him and saw he was locked in a pensive mood.

"Sobering thought," the young Cockney said after awhile.

Rex wondered if he should broach the subject of Rosie and the will—but if Charley had no knowledge of it, he didn't want to stir the marital pot by bringing it up. He uncorked the bottle of port and poured a measure into Charley's glass.

"I like Anthony for the murders," the young man said, impersonating a New York City cop. "Not because he's a pouf or anything like that," he added in his usual voice. "I think well enough of Patrick—but Anthony comes across as more evil than anyone else here."

"That's no indication. Ted Bundy was highly personable and the Ken and Barbie Murderers in Canada were a normal-seeming young couple."

"Still, Anthony was in the kitchen when Miriam went in. Who's to say he was down in the cellar?"

"Aye, he is the most probable suspect in that murder."

"Patrick was in Wanda's room and could've found the key and given it to Anthony."

"But where are your supporting facts? You canna make them up just to fit your theory. Hercule Poirot would say to look for the *facts*."

"Who's he when he's at home?"

"The little Belgian detective in the Agatha Christie novels."

"So you read that stuff, do you?"

"My mother does. As apparently does Mrs. Smithings, judging by the books in the library."

"A guest could have left those books. I saw a Jackie Collins in the library, and I'm sure Mrs. Smithings doesn't read raunchy novels. The one time she had to have done it to produce Rodney, she probably lay back and thought of England, wishing the Colonel would hurry up and get it over with."

Chuckling at the picture Charley conjured up, Rex filled his pipe from the leather tobacco pouch. "I'm sure when they were newlyweds they spent a lot of time in their room, just like you and Yvette—emerging in the radiant aftermath as though they had discovered delights known only to themselves," he added poetically.

"You're not past it yourself, you know. Don't you and the fair Helen have a thing going?"

"Charley, lad, even if we were, I wouldna tell you."

"*Noblesse oblige?*"

"Exactly. And, anyway, we're not."

"Do you think it's a psychopathic serial killer?" Charley asked in the *non sequitur* way of people idling away time.

"Either way, after the first murder, the second is easier."

Charley sat forward, cradling his tumbler of port. "Do you speak from professional experience?"

"Aye."

Charley sprawled back on the sofa. "You know, I'm trying to imagine you prosecuting your victims. Do you wear a wig?"

"As a matter of fact, I do. And black silk robes."

Charley laughed. "How long have you been a barrister? I mean, advocate?"

"I was appointed Queen's Counsel three years ago and was admitted to the Scottish Bar eighteen years before that."

"Blimey. Have you ever thought about doing anything else?"

"Aye. I'd like to run a small bar in a not-so touristy part of Spain. Perhaps I'll do that in my retirement." Why was he telling Charley his private fantasies? It must be the port. "But I'd never admit that to my mother. She doesn't approve of alcohol, especially since my father was killed by a drunk driver."

Charley shook his head slowly. "That's terrible. My mum didn't want me to be a firefighter, but I did that for a while before becoming a paramedic."

Rex stared into his glass. "I wanted to be a firefighter when I was a lad."

"What boy doesn't? I suppose it's too late for you to do that now, but there's always that bar in Spain to look forward to."

"Aye. Or perhaps Florida."

"I'll join you, mate."

A companionable silence fell between them as they gazed into the dancing flames. At some point in the conversation, Rex drifted off into slumber. In his dream, he saw a chipper Mr. Lawdry at one of the games tables on the far side of the room shooting winks into a cup with Yvette. Miriam Greenbaum poured over her manuscript on the sofa, while Wanda sat across from her, legs folded sideways, filing her nails. They appeared as shadows, shades of the

Underworld, and then metamorphosed into an ancient funeral pyre spouting flames.

A log cracking in the fire jogged him awake. "Do you think this house is haunted, Charley?" he asked, resuming his vigil.

The young man stirred, eyes fluttering open. "What? Ghosts?"

"Uneasy spirits coming back to claim their time and space?"

Charley scoffed. "I don't believe in ghosts."

"Aye, but can you discount them so readily? 'There are more things in heaven and earth, Horatio, than are dreamt of in your philosophy.'"

"Well, Hamlet couldn't make up his mind about anything, could he?"

"True enough."

Presently, Rex heard the stairs creak. He tensed in his chair. Steps approached down the carpeted hall, followed by a woman's hoarse cough. He stretched out his left arm; the cuff of his sweater receded up his wrist revealing his watch: 5:30.

"Mrs. Bellows, getting up early to put the turkey in the oven," Charley murmured. "I heard it was over 28 pounds. She'll be basting all morning." He yawned. "D'you think she knows about the fire? She must have smelt the smoke up on the landing."

"Most of the smoke will have gone out the window by now. The whole hotel could have burned down except that the carpet was doused in water around the bed. That's what caused so much smoke."

"Someone made sure the smoke alarm wouldn't go off. The person who murdered Henry probably realized the fuzz would be along soon now that the snow's let up, and didn't want to take any chances with them finding cyanide in his system."

Rex relit his pipe. "Could be the same pyromaniac who burned the manuscript. I found Patrick's matches on Lawdry's bed. No doubt they were supposed to burn too."

"How do you know they're Patrick's?"

"The box has red paint on it." Rex drew it from his pocket and licked his finger. "It's watercolour and comes off easily." He showed Charley the red residue on his skin—the same shade as the robin's breast.

"How was the fire fueled? Did you smell petrol?"

"No," Rex said. "Would alcohol leave a smell?"

"Not if it burned."

"I haven't prosecuted any domestic arson cases, only large-scale fires. The culprits all knew what they were doing—though they obviously weren't clever enough to avoid getting caught."

"Wonder if this one will be clever enough."

"It has to be someone who cared enough about the hotel, or maybe just themselves, not to want to let it burn to the ground."

"An expert in fine art and antiques like Anthony wouldn't want to destroy a Victorian manor that has most of the original furniture in it. He might try to control the fire by drenching the area around the bed with water—especially if he and Patrick have designs on the place. Just the other day, they were talking about what changes they'd like to make."

"I see your mind's still made up aboot Anthony. Well, I think I'll go and see if I can rustle up a cup of tea. D'ye want any?"

"Nah, mate. I think I'll hit the sack. You going to stay up?"

"Aye. I couldna get a wink o' sleep now if I tried." Rex finished the last drop of port in his tumbler and rose from the armchair.

His back felt stiff. Charley was right: his days of ever fighting fires for a living were over.

———

"May I trouble you for a cup of tea, Mrs. Bellows?"

"It'd be no trouble at all," the cook said. "I was going to make one for myself just as soon as I get this bird in the oven. There we go." She closed the stainless steel door on the biggest turkey Rex had ever seen, dotted with pats of butter, liberally seasoned, and wearing what looked like miniature chef's hats on its feet.

"That must have taken a ton of stuffing."

"A ton is about right. Sage, onion and sausage. And chestnut puree on the side."

"You've done us proud." Rex stepped out of her way as she filled the kettle.

Mrs. Bellows opened a tea caddy decorated with a blue willow pattern. "There should be plenty of leftovers. I like to make curry fricassee with the turkey the day after Christmas." She arranged the mugs, teapot, and strainer on the pine table. "I'll just fetch the milk."

As she returned carrying a small jug, Rex brought his mug to his lips and sniffed. "I put a bit of this white powder in my tea," he said, indicating a canister on the table. "It may be table salt, and I'm allergic. Could you taste it for me?"

"Oh, my fault—I forgot the sugar bowl." Without hesitation, Mrs. Bellows took a sip of his tea. "It's sugar," she said, sitting down. "Though I've no idea what it's doing in that container. Rosie has been reorganizing things again, I shouldn't wonder."

The container was the one Charley had found in the trash. Rex had smuggled it into the kitchen and sprinkled a small packet of sugar from the train into his mug, curious to see if the cook would be willing to taste the sweetened tea.

"If you have an allergy to table salt, you best take care," she remarked. "I use a lot in my cooking."

"I take anti-allergy pills," Rex fabricated. "I just haven't got around to taking one today."

"It is still early," the cook agreed. She took a hearty swallow and let out a sigh of contentment. "Nothing like a good cuppa to set you up for the day."

"Mrs. Bellows," Rex began tentatively. "I'm curious why you didn't mention the terrorist bombings in London the other night when we were talking about Rosie's sister. It was only after I saw a reference to the attacks in the paper and tied them to the date the barman mentioned at the pub that I put two and two together."

"We're not supposed to talk religion or politics. It's one of the rules. Mrs. Smithings says you never know if a guest might be listening and take offense."

"The bombings were a national disaster transcending religion and politics."

"I know, but Rosie feels very bitter about it, so I don't bring it up. Having your twin taken away like that must feel like losing half of yourself."

"An identical twin?"

Sandy Bellows nodded and gave a heavy sigh. Rex mentally slapped his forehead. Those photos in Rosie's room were not of her, but of her twin sister.

"Very competent, Marie was," Mrs. Bellows was saying. "Practically had the run of the place. It was the explosion on the train in Edgware Road Station that killed her. Personally, I don't care if people are Muslim, Jewish, or gay; Labour, Liberal, or Conservative, just as long as they don't take innocent lives. There's just good people and there's bad people in my opinion."

"Those are my sentiments as well, Mrs. Bellows."

"The young Londoner staying here—Charley, I think his name is—Rosie told me his cousin got his legs blown off in the bus bombing." She heaved herself out of her chair. "Oh, me old bones. I feel every one of my fifty-five years on cold mornings."

Rex watched as she rinsed out her mug at the sink. "Do you use much alcohol in your cooking?"

"What a funny question! I never met a bunch of guests so interested in what went into their food. Alcohol tarts things up, it does. Let's see now. I put kirsch in the fruit salad and rum in the Christmas pudding. And wine in the Chicken Marsala. Then there's…"

Rex finished his tea and drifted toward the pantry. "Ah, this is where you keep your liqueur, I see. Is any missing?"

Brushing her hands on her apron, Mrs. Bellows charged toward him. "Has that old good-for-nothing been at my bottles again?" she demanded, scanning the shelf with a suspicious eye. "Well, the bottles *look* the same as I left them yesterday afternoon. I check every day, just in case."

"I gave Clifford a gift of sherry yesterday, so your stock is probably safe for now."

"Hmph. I should lock that pantry, but it's one extra thing to remember, and I have enough to do as it is. Well, I best get on," she said, hastening back to her double oven. "There'll be seven at table and then the staff will have theirs."

Apparently, Mrs. Bellows still didn't know about Wanda's murder, and she hadn't mentioned the fire. Rex closed the pantry door. Who else had access to inflammatory booze? He had found brandy in Anthony's suite the night he searched the guest rooms. Just then, he heard Clifford at the scullery door, stomping the snow off his boots.

"Could you unlock the door for him?" Mrs. Bellows called. "I'm up to my elbows in flour."

Rex let the old man in with a jovial greeting. Outside, a feeble light accompanied the crisp clean air. "Clifford, you mentioned a *twitten* yesterday."

"Ar."

"Show me."

"Now? I just got the snow off me boots an' eh be freezin' to death."

"Ah, now, it's no as cold as it's been. Did you enjoy the sherry we got for you? I'll vouch it's better than the brand Mrs. Smithings serves."

Clifford grudgingly admitted it was and stepped back out the door, leading Rex beneath the eaves toward the east wing. All of a sudden, a scraping of iron jarred above Rex's head. Springing away from the wall, he looked up and saw a pair of black-clad arms fling open the windowpanes. "What a glorious Christmas morning, Reginald," Mrs. Smithings cawed down at him. "It will feel so good to air the rooms at last."

Rex could not help but think of the two open windows upstairs airing dead bodies—while poor Ms. Greenbaum had to make do with a dank cellar. "Merry Christmas," he greeted Mrs. Smithings, thinking he would have raised his hat if he had one.

He followed after Clifford who had scuttled out of sight of the window when he heard Mrs. Smithings' voice. Upon reaching the corner, Rex stopped in surprise. Along the side of the house ran a double yew hedge. Had he not been interrupted by the argument in the honeymoon suite the preceding morning, he might have seen it from the arched window on the upstairs landing.

The hedge rose to his shoulder, the earth between the rows protected from snow by a canopy of leaves. Exiting the hedge, someone could look in the kitchen window and see the entire room. Stooping, Rex made his way through the leafy tunnel. Before he came to the other end, he passed a thinning patch in the hedge and looking out, saw that he was parallel to the library. He had forgotten about the exterior library door. When he'd been in the room, the curtains had been drawn over the door and windows. The door led out onto a small patio presided over by an Apollo on a sundial, which had fascinated him as a boy.

Too large to fit through the hole in the hedge, he continued to the end and trudged back to the library. The door had been pushed back at some point, leaving an angle of flattened snow and enough room for a person to pass through the gap.

"Clifford, are you sure no one entered the scullery from outside two days ago when you were at the sherry?"

Lines furrowed the old man's brow beneath the misshapen brown cap. "Ar, but I didn't see who 'twas. I was 'id in the coats and 'twas all but dark."

"Why didn't you tell me that before?"

"You didn't ask. You asked who was in the kitchen."

"That's right." Rex thought for a moment. "I had no reason to suspect someone had come through that door—I didn't know about the hedge then. Did you hear anyone leave?"

"I don' remember. I heard a cross voice and a *whump*."

And Miriam Greenbaum went tumbling down the stairs...

"All right, Clifford, let's get back inside."

They retraced their way to the scullery.

"Is the dog still doing fine?" Rex asked, wiping his shoes on the mat.

"Ar. Ee's a good dog an' 'ardly ever barks."

"Good. I was worried about that."

Rex passed Rosie in the kitchen. "You're up bright and early this Christmas morning."

"I have to help Mrs. Bellows." The girl tied an apron around her hourglass figure. "Can't go letting her do it all by herself, can I?"

"You're a love," the cook told her, turning around from the countertop, rolling pin in hand.

Rex found a clean cup on the drainer and poured tea from the pot to take up to Helen. In spite of the anticipatory spring in his step, he managed not to spill any on his way down the hall.

No sooner had he placed his foot on the first step of the stairs than screams arose from the kitchen.

FOURTEEN

DROPPING THE TEA, REX ran back to the kitchen wondering what new horror had befallen. He found Rosie hobbling to a chair at the pine table, bleeding at the knee where her black woolen stocking was torn. "What happened?" he asked.

"Clifford tried to kill me, that's what. I tripped on the axe he left half buried in the snow. He did it on purpose. And he came after me with it! He was trying to kill me, the crazy old coot!"

"Warn't!" Clifford said, hovering, cap in hand.

Mrs. Bellows examined Rosie's knee. "That's a nasty graze you have there. Let me get some disinfectant."

"I just went out to feed the robin some crumbs. Ouch!" Rosie gasped as the cook dabbed a soapy paper towel on her cuts.

"He *is* a menace the way he leaves his axe lying around," the older woman agreed. "Only a matter of time before there was an accident. There you go, dear. Best put a plaster on it."

Rex addressed Clifford. "Did you attack Rosie?"

"Nar. Why would I do that? Eh likes Rosie well enough. Eh just picked up the axe to move it out the way."

"Sandy, why don't you tell Mr. Graves what happened to Clifford's wife?" Rosie said. "Go on."

Mrs. Bellows faced Rex, her glance slipping to the old man. "Well, I don't know that it's any of my business, and it was a long time ago, but there was talk of him pushing his wife down the well."

"Nar! She fell!"

"Aye. I heard the story, but the police couldn't prove Clifford was responsible."

"Well, I didn't know if you knew, but what with that American woman getting pushed down the cellar steps, I thought I should mention it."

"I appreciate it, Mrs. Bellows."

"Lies!" Clifford cried, retreating toward the scullery.

The cook stuck her hands on her hips, watching him until he disappeared. "I ask you, have you ever seen the like? Skulking in the scullery like some weasel and popping out when you least expect it! Makes you wonder all the same ..." She looked askance at the cellar door. "When are they going to come for the body?"

"Some time today, I think. Can you walk, Rosie?" Rex helped her to her feet.

"Ow. It still hurts a bit," the girl said, limping toward the sink. "Shall I start on the breakfast, Sandy?"

"It's just bacon, black pudding, and eggs this morning. And make some porridge, dear. I'll start my cranberry sauce and then help you."

169

Fresh tea in hand, Rex left them to their preparations. In the foyer, he heard Mrs. Smithings' voice up on the landing.

"Merry Christmas, Mr. Vance."

"To you too, Mrs. Smithings."

A man's brisk steps proceeded down the stairs. Patrick was just the person he wanted to see. Rex veered toward the drawing room and took a seat, casually drinking the tea meant for Helen. The poor woman would never get her tea at this rate. Patrick ventured into the room, his eyes searching the furniture.

"Is this what you're looking for?" Rex tossed him the box of matches he had found in Lawdry's room.

"What happened to this?" Patrick asked, turning the charred box around in his pale hands. "Did you find it in the fireplace?"

"No, upstairs."

Patrick looked surprised. "I only smoke down here. I leave the matches on this end table."

"Someone must have borrowed them." Rex paused for a second. "I wanted to ask you if Wanda told you anything of interest the other night."

"Like what?"

"Gossip about someone at the hotel—anything at all. I'm sure you were both chatting away about this and that while you were doing her hair."

"Oh. Well, we discussed celebrities and the latest on Charles and Camilla. We did compare notes on the murders, but it turned out we had different ideas about that."

Rex tapped his silver teaspoon dry against the rim of his cup. For some reason, the action brought back the other night when he'd helped himself to sugar from Rosie's coffee tray as Helen,

Wanda, and the Perkins sat at the card table waiting for him to dust the candlesticks for fingerprints. "Wanda wrote in her diary that you both *argued* about who murdered Miriam," he prodded Patrick Vance.

"It was more of a heated debate. I said I was putting my money on Clifford, and she hinted that Anthony might have done it, which set me off a little—I mean, he feels bad enough about how he treated Miriam without people thinking he killed her. Anthony wouldn't kill the proverbial fly."

"Did Wanda talk about Rosie?"

"She only said she saw Rosie and Charley kissing in the library and that he was playing with fire because Yvette was the viciously jealous type. He didn't waste much time, did he?"

"Not if it's true." Rex asked Patrick if he'd come across a labeled key in Wanda's room and he denied it.

"Her hair was so soft and supple." Patrick held his hands palm upward, elegant fingers spread and slightly curled as though reliving the feel of it.

"Can I see your sketchpad a minute?" Rex asked, interrupting the young man's reverie.

Patrick retrieved it. "Why?"

"I seem to remember seeing something of interest that didn't register at the time."

Rex turned to the Christmas tree scene in the pad and studied the arrangement of tea items on the round Victorian table. The teapot, sugar bowl, milk jug, cups and saucers, and a pile of side plates were set up to the left of the table, along with a tiered cake tray. The coffee carafe was relegated to the right, together with a cream jug, cup, saucer, and plate. Judging from the perspective of the scene, Patrick had sketched it from this very chair.

"This picture of Anthony and the two women, with the tree in the background ... is that a tray under the coffee carafe?"

Patrick leaned over his shoulder. "Yes. It's the black lacquer tray you displayed the fingerprints on."

"Was it on that table?"

"It must have been, otherwise I wouldn't have sketched it in," Patrick replied touchily.

Rex held up the pad. "Is that a smudge on top of the plate?"

"No, it's a tart. Does that help you?"

"It's a starting point. If I follow my theory, it may lead me to the end of the maze."

"Mind if I get my breakfast now?"

Rex accompanied Patrick into the dining room to fetch a third cup of tea for Helen. Mrs. Smithings, arranging a vase of holly with clusters of blood-red berries, looked up from the table as they entered.

"You were out early this morning, Reginald. Did you enjoy your walk?"

"Most pleasant. I don't remember the yew hedge being there before."

"There used to be a rose garden, but the blooms did not do well on that side of the house. Too much shade."

Rex filled his cup. "Did you get the missing key back, Mrs. Smithings?"

"Yes. It was sitting on my desk this morning. I must have put it there and forgotten all about it."

He left the dining room and mounted the stairs, holding the saucer over the cup to keep the tea hot. He knocked on the door to his room. "Helen? It's Rex."

"Just a minute." Four minutes later, Helen opened the door, wrapped in her shawl. "Sorry to keep you waiting."

Rex detected a whiff of minty toothpaste on her breath. And she was wearing the swan earrings. She ran back to bed and buried herself under the covers. "Brrr."

"I'll get the fire going," he said, depositing the cup on the bedside table.

Helen resurfaced, her hair in charming disarray, and propped up the pillows. "A fire would be lovely. And thanks for the tea. What have you been doing all this time? It's past eight o'clock."

Rex blew on the fledgling fire and added a birch log, wiping the palms of his hand on his trousers as he got to his feet. "I think I found the last piece of the puzzle and now I have the whole picture. No a verra pretty picture, mind."

"Rex! You genius. Tell me!"

"I'd rather you heard my brilliant summation, which I plan to give after breakfast downstairs."

"You are such a spoilsport, do you know that?"

"Aye, so I've been told." He extracted a plaid packet of shortbread fingers from his suitcase. "Here, have one of these with your tea." He sat down on the side of the bed.

"Oh, I love shortbread." She took a dimpled block of buttery biscuit and nibbled on it, brushing the crumbs off the quilt. "You make a delicious cup of tea. I wish there was more."

"I hope you're not suggesting I traipse all the way back down the stairs."

"No. Just curious to see if you would, that's all."

"I might, but you need to get up and dressed, young lady."

"'Young lady.' I like that."

If you only knew the trouble I went to, getting you that cup, he thought.

Helen licked her thumb and finger, and stretched luxuriously. "When I'm with you, I forget all the bad stuff that's happened. I even forgot about Wanda for a while just now."

"And I like seeing you all cosy in my bed, but we can't ignore the outside world."

"Worst luck." Her foot stole out from beneath the covers and caressed his thigh.

"Wickedness."

"Prude."

He tapped her on the nose. "I'll see you downstairs."

"You don't get off that easily." She pulled a sprig of mistletoe from under the pillow. "If I don't get a kiss, I'll feel like Wanda stole you, just like she did Paul."

Rex leaned forward. "Merry Christmas, Helen."

"Merry Christmas—Rex."

He kissed her warm lips, lingered a second, and withdrew. Her eyes smiled at him. He jumped off the bed. "I'm gone!"

Once on the landing, he continued along the east wing. Hoping the hotel proprietor was still downstairs, he crossed to her suite and entered with a perfunctory knock. The essence of Mrs. Smithings breathed in these rooms. He had not noticed it as much the other night when the cook had been with him. He felt the weight of dread on his heart, as though he had spiraled backward in time and were standing in a forbidden place, his socks rumpling down his shins, sweat on his palms—fearful of some dire punishment, yet rooted to the spot by something bigger than fear.

By and by, the spell was broken. He pulled himself together, amazed that as a boy he had been intimidated by Dahlia Smithings, a formidable and handsome woman back then, now a frail creature who'd suffered through the deaths of her husband and only child and struggled to hold on to her family home on her own. She no longer held sway over him. The clumsy schoolboy was gone.

The ornamental clock on the mantelpiece pointed to ten. As on his last visit, an eerie, almost sepulchral quiet reigned in her room, everything just as before—except that time can never go back, nor can it stand still.

FIFTEEN

As REX PASSED THE honeymoon suite on his way back from Mrs. Smithings' rooms, Yvette slipped out the door.

"Charley's out like a light," she whispered. "How late were you up talking?"

"All night."

She drew him away from the suite. "Did you and Charley have a heart to heart?"

"I suppose so. I remember telling him some of my foolish dreams, at any rate."

"Did he—did he mention anything in particular? I mean, about us?"

Rex knew better than to volunteer information.

"Oh, I might as well tell you," she blurted. "We're going to have a baby."

"Congratulations."

"Charley's not happy about it. He's trying to put a brave face on it now, but he was really angry when he found out. I wasn't as careful as I should have been."

"It takes two to tango. If he was that concerned about a baby, he could have taken precautions himself."

Yvette's face cleared. "You're right. You know, when I first saw you, I thought you were a bit of a fuddy-duddy. But you're not like that at all."

"A fuddy-duddy? I'll have to change my image. I've already been called a prude this morning."

Yvette giggled as they started down the stairs. "I can't wait to get home to my mum's to break the news. I just know she's going to be thrilled to death. Oh," the young woman exclaimed, pausing on the step, "I suppose we can't say things like that any more. It does sound so flip when you think about it."

"Aye, but the situation should be resolved shortly."

When they reached the dining room, Patrick was still at breakfast. Anthony had joined him.

"Morning, morning," the interior designer said. "Where are Helen and Charley?"

"Helen will be down in a minute," Rex replied as Yvette filled her plate at the buffet. "Charley's still asleep."

"We all survived the night then," Anthony remarked. "And hopefully, we'll make it through the day. I'm avoiding anything that remotely smells of almonds."

Mrs. Bellows entered the room and placed a dish on a heating tray. "Just in time for your porridge," she told Rex.

"Thank you, Mrs. Bellows." He ladled the steaming oatmeal into a bowl. "Would you be kind enough to ask the rest of the staff to join the guests in the drawing room at nine thirty?"

She cast him a wary glance. "Right you are, Mr. Graves."

"What's happening at nine thirty?" Anthony asked as the cook left.

"The villain will be unmasked," Patrick said.

"Really?" Anthony turned to Rex. "Who?"

"Wait and see."

Yvette stared at the cooked breakfast in front of her. "I don't think I can eat this." Upturning her chair in her haste, she ran out of the room.

"What's the matter with her?"

"She's pregnant."

"Ah." Anthony spread marmalade on his wheat toast. "I thought it might be nerves. I'm pretty shaken up myself. After the fire last night, I wouldn't have slept two winks if Patrick hadn't given me some of his Valerian."

"And two shots of brandy," Patrick added.

Anthony shook his head. "I don't know how I got through that bottle so quickly. It was half full just the other day."

Rex drew his own conclusions from that, but said nothing. All would be revealed soon enough.

———

Hands clasped behind his back, Rex stood by the mantelpiece in the drawing room, trying to anticipate every eventuality that might arise from his revelations. There was no easy way to approach this, he decided.

Patrick and Anthony arrived first.

"Nine twenty," Anthony said, glancing at his watch. "We thought we'd bag the best seats. Where should we sit?"

Rex swept his hand around the room. "Anywhere you wish."

Anthony selected his favorite armchair by the fire and crossed his legs, rubbing his obsidian ring in circular motions. Patrick went to open a window and stood there smoking. Helen entered with her knitting and settled herself on a sofa without a word. The click of needles distracted Rex from his thoughts. Yvette dragged a bleary-eyed Charley into the room. He must have slept in his clothes, judging by their crumpled appearance.

Charley collapsed into the loveseat. "I feel like death warmed up," he moaned. "I don't think port agrees with me."

"I'll bring you a cup of coffee," Yvette said soothingly.

Mrs. Bellows and Rosie appeared.

"Come on in," Rex said. "There's plenty of room on the sofa."

They sat opposite Helen. He had never before seen Mrs. Bellows without her apron. She wore a dark blue dress and looked about the room expectantly. Nobody spoke. Clifford shuffled in next with the puppy, which bounded up to Rex with little whines of excitement. Rosie fed it a sugar lump and it settled down at her feet.

"Are we all here?" Mrs. Smithings demanded, making her entrance in black crepe, the signature pearls at her throat.

"We're just waiting for Yvette."

The newlywed came in soon after and handed Charley his coffee. She sat down beside him, hands twitching in the lap of her jeans.

Rex surveyed the room, feeling more exposed than at court where he could hide behind the costume, props, and setting that lent his performance a theatrical air, and where the audience judged him solely on the merits of his prosecutorial skills. The faces that gazed up at him now were no less curious and intense than those in a jury box.

As he cleared his throat in preparation for his speech, he tried not to look at Mrs. Smithings, who was no doubt scrutinizing him with a critical eye. "I have called you all here to review the sinister events of the past few days—"

"Before we commence, Reginald, I want to present you with your gift," Mrs. Smithings said. "It is, after all, Christmas Day and you have worked very hard in trying to solve this case."

"Er, thank you, Mrs. Smithings," he said, breaking his concentration and accepting a long object wrapped in red and green paper.

"It was Rodney's hunting rifle," she said as he tore off the wrapping. "I would like you to have it."

"I don't know what to say." He truly didn't—the thought of all the defenseless creatures Rodney had killed with this gun was abhorrent, yet how could he refuse?

"Looks like a Holland & Holland double rifle, late 1800s," Anthony observed. "May I see?"

Rex handed it over to him. "I didn't check to see if it was loaded," he said, turning to Mrs. Smithings.

"Of course it's not."

Anthony held it in both hands, examining it every which way. "A beautiful piece—mint condition. Just look at this exquisite walnut wood engraved with the 'Royal' scroll."

"It belonged to Rodney's great-grandfather. My son took the very best care of it, and it shoots true."

"Thank you again, Mrs. Smithings," Rex said. "I will treasure it. Now then, not to postpone the proceedings further, I shall give a brief review of the facts for the benefit of those who may not be entirely familiar with them." He lifted one finger. "First, on December twenty-second, Henry Lawdry died in this room. Sodium cyanide poisoning was found in his iced almond tart—"

A few gasps escaped in the room.

"…though death by cyanide has yet to be corroborated by a medical examination. Second, on December twenty-third, Miriam Greenbaum fell to her death in the cellar. We can assume the murder weapon to be the silver candlestick. There would be no reason otherwise to wipe it clean of prints. Third, on December twenty-fourth, Wanda Martyr was found suffocated in her bed."

A stifled exclamation from Mrs. Bellows ensued.

"The attempt to burn Mr. Lawdry's body late last night also points to foul play," Rex went on. "Yet I could find no motive for his murder beyond an antique cameo brooch that he allegedly gave to Yvette Perkins and which Wanda Martyr claimed as her due. Following motive, we look at means and opportunity. Almost anyone present in this room had the means and opportunity to poison the almond tart presumed to have killed Mr. Lawdry. The question is, how did it find its way onto his plate?

"Anthony was the first to serve himself tea the afternoon Lawdry died. According to the cook, he was in and out of the kitchen.

He could have doctored the tart. The next day, when Ms. Greenbaum entered the kitchen, he was already there, candlestick at hand."

"You're out of your mind!" Anthony declared, his face an angry shade of puce.

Rex continued undeterred. "Wanda found out from Anthony that Yvette had the brooch. She may have suspected Yvette of Lawdry's murder, perhaps in collusion with her husband, who after all has medical knowledge and could have introduced the hypothesis of cyanide to cover up the real cause of death. Since Charley was not in the room when Lawdry died, he was never suspected. I might add that Charley was a firefighter, and thus has professional knowledge of fires. And nobody knows for sure where the couple was when Ms. Greenbaum met her end on the cellar floor."

"You don't really believe that, do you?" the Cockney asked, jolted into an upright position on the loveseat. "How would we have entered Wanda's room?"

Rex ignored the questions. "Patrick was possibly the last person to see Wanda alive. He argued with her in her room and could have taken the master key she stole from Rosie, returning the next morning. He was the first to reach Lawdry when the old man had his attack. And his matches were found in the deceased's room after the fire…"

Patrick threw his cigarette butt out the window in a gesture of disdain. "You're going to accuse Helen next. She had access to Wanda's room through the adjoining door and could have killed her just before she went to the village with you—perfect alibi. And she could just as easily have murdered Miriam after she followed her out of the dining room."

Helen looked anxiously at Rex.

"Aye, Patrick, what you say is logical enough. Now let's consider the staff. Mrs. Bellows prepared the almond tarts; in fact, they were her own recipe. She could have spiked one of them. We only have her word for it that she was powdering her nose when Ms. Greenbaum went into the kitchen. Sandy Bellows is not only a trained nurse with pharmaceutical experience, but a woman of considerable strength who could have suffocated Wanda Martyr without any difficulty at all."

Rex swung toward the cook on the sofa and found her gazing up at him quite impassively. Next, he turned his attention to the odd-job man cringing against the far wall. "Clifford helped Mrs. Bellows out in the kitchen. Perhaps it was not cyanide that killed Mr. Lawdry, but rat poison. Clifford was in the vicinity when Ms. Greenbaum went to fetch the dog from the cellar. He was suspected of pushing his wife to her death ten years ago. And he went up to the attic for ski equipment at around the time Wanda Martyr was murdered."

Rex put up a hand before Clifford could protest. "These are plausible arguments, but when considering all three murders with regard to any of the aforementioned suspects, none are satisfactory. Only two people working in tandem could have committed all four crimes, including setting fire to Mr. Lawdry's corpse.

"The burning of the body brought me back to the burning of the manuscript. Whereas the burning of the body appeared to be an attempt to conceal evidence, the burning of the manuscript spelt rage. Who would have been most enraged by a biography on President Bush? It was only when I studied Patrick's sketch that my suspicion was confirmed: Henry was not the intended victim, but Miriam Greenbaum all along."

"How d'you make that out?" Patrick asked.

"Miriam was the only guest to drink coffee at teatime. A single plate was set out beside the carafe. It would be natural for Miriam to take that plate—but the doddery old Mr. Lawdry served himself first, not realizing his error until he sat down and tasted the coffee. By then, it was too late. He had already taken the almond tart put aside for Miriam on the coffee tray.

"Usually in a case we ask ourselves, 'Who had most to gain?' In this case, we should ask ourselves, 'Who had the most to lose?' In fact, who *had* lost the most?" Rex let the weight of his words sink in as his eyes circled the hushed audience.

"Are you going to keep us in suspense much longer?" Anthony demanded.

Rex gave a dramatic pause. "I put it to you that Mrs. Smithings laced the tart with cyanide and instructed Rosie to put it on Ms. Greenbaum's plate—"

"Mrs. Smithings?" Charley cried. "And Rosie? Never!"

"Shows *you*, doesn't it?" Yvette said with smug satisfaction.

"I was in the drawing room when Ms. Greenbaum died," Rosie protested. "Helen saw me. You can't pin that on me."

"Let me finish," Rex said. "With a well-timed blow of the candlestick, Mrs. Smithings knocked Miriam off balance, and the literary agent fell down the cellar steps to her death. In spite of, or by virtue of, her rheumatoid arthritis pills, Mrs. Smithings had adequate strength and range of motion to accomplish this feat. I saw her vigorously push open the large windows of her suite only this morning. She did not, however, have the strength to kill Wanda Martyr."

"Oh, blimey. I never thought…," Cook mumbled as Rex pressed on.

"Wanda was under the impression that Yvette had put the brooch in the library safe. Using Rosie's master key, she opened the safe and discovered not the brooch but Mrs. Smithings' will bequeathing Swanmere Manor to Rosie. This made her suspicious. She mentioned in her diary that Rosie had been acting guiltily ever since Lawdry played Tiddlywinks with Yvette before tea. That is, from around the time he died, Rosie's attitude changed. Was she feeling guilt over his murder, or guilt over flirting with Charley in the library? Most likely the former.

"As best as I can reconstruct, Wanda confronted Rosie when the girl came in to clean yesterday morning. Rosie said she went in at about eleven and left when she saw the guest was still asleep. Rosie would have known from the note Helen left Wanda that Helen would be away from the hotel for a while. We canna be exactly sure when she went in, but by the time she left, Wanda was dead. Whatever Wanda told her, it was enough to make Rosie panic and smother her to death. Not only did Rosie fear being implicated in Lawdry's murder, she was afraid she wouldna inherit the hotel.

"Rosie retrieved her key from Wanda's room. Caught off guard when I asked her about it, she denied having it. Mrs. Smithings tried to cover up for her by saying the missing key inexplicably turned up on her desk this morning, when in fact it was in the safe last night where she locked it up. Only Mrs. Smithings had access to Lawdry's room. She went in to cover up evidence of poisoning by setting fire to his bed. She knew the police would be here this morning—because I told her." He hazarded a glance at Mrs. Smithings, who fixed him with a steely glare.

"I admit to murdering the American," she declared.

"She's crazy!" Patrick exclaimed from the window.

"Crazy with grief," Rex explained. "She felt George W. Bush was personally responsible for her son's death. Rodney Smithings was killed in southern Iraq when his convoy was ambushed, and Ms. Greenbaum was unfortunate enough to have been working on getting the president's biography published. Mrs. Smithings' destruction of the manuscript and murder of the literary agent were acts of vindication. As for Rosie—she lost her sister in a terrorist bombing launched in retaliation to the war. She and Mrs. Smithings were kindred spirits in crisis."

"A lot of people lost relatives in the London bombings," Rosie replied bitterly. "Anyway, Mrs. Smithings was in her suite when the American woman died. No one saw her downstairs."

"Mrs. Smithings entered the kitchen through the outside door to the scullery, as I discovered this morning. I already had my suspicions regarding her involvement. From the start, she was curiously tight-lipped about her son's death and yet her room is a shrine to his memory. The clock stopped at ten o'clock on the fourteenth of September, 2004. Am I right, Mrs. Smithings?"

"As always, Reginald."

"We never meant to hurt poor old Henry," Rosie burst out.

"Henry was a casualty of war," Mrs. Smithings shrilled. "And it was probably a blessing for him. He was alone, as am I."

"Escort Mrs. Smithings to her private quarters, please, Charley. We'll lock Rosie in the office."

Before anyone had time to react, Rosie grabbed the hunting rifle from Anthony's hands and backed out of the room. "It *is* loaded, you know. Nobody move or I'll shoot!"

SIXTEEN

Rosie crouched over the gun, her dark eyes reflecting the desperation of a cornered animal. Everyone in the drawing room froze. The solid French doors leading into the hall banged shut behind her. Rex ran toward them and wrenched one open, unable to tell in which direction she had gone. Not having heard the front door, he chased across the foyer and into the library. Lucky guess. The outside door stood ajar. Passing through it, he almost slipped on the hardened snow. He righted himself and looked up and down the alley between the house and the yew hedge. The dog, which had followed him, yelped in a frenzy of excitement at his feet.

"Seek," he coaxed. "Go find." Rex ran the length of the yew hedge, guessing that Rosie was hiding in there. He knew he wouldn't be able to catch up with her if he went inside. She was more nimble in spite of her injury, the extent of which he suspected she'd exaggerated.

The dog, doubtless thinking this was a game and remembering the sugar lumps Rosie had fed him, burrowed under the hedge and began barking, giving away her position. The branches of the hedge quivered as she fled toward the back of the house.

Skidding and sliding, Rex sprinted to the end of the tunnel and caught her as she flew out. He wrested the gun off her. "It's over, Rosie," he said. "Come back inside out of the cold."

She eluded his grip and sank wailing into the snow, as the dog nuzzled into her pockets. "I don't want to go to prison," she sobbed. "My parents won't be able to afford a good defense."

"I have a colleague who is a partner in one of the best criminal defense firms in London. I'll talk to him." Rex pulled her to her feet and took her back to the house. Voices rang out from the front and back of the hotel. "I have her!" he yelled, dragging her through the library door.

"All I did was put the almond tart on the American's plate. I didn't add the poison."

"And Wanda Martyr?"

"I had to do it. She was too nosy. She would have ruined everything."

"*Abyssus abyssum invocat.*"

"Excuse me?"

"One wrongdoing causes another."

"But that's it, I swear! I had nothing to do with Ms. Greenbaum's death and I didn't burn poor old Mr. Lawdry."

"Did you take the brandy from Anthony's room?"

"Mrs. Smithings asked if I knew where there was something to help burn the evidence. She never said what evidence. If I'd taken anything from Sandy's pantry, she would have noticed."

Rex locked the exterior door after them, with one eye on Rosie to make sure she didn't bolt from the room. Anthony and Patrick appeared in the doorway.

"We'd better tie her to a chair in the office until the police get here," Rex told them. "I'll have Clifford fetch some rope." He delivered the girl into their custody and went to check on Mrs. Smithings, who was in Charley's care.

"She insisted on being left alone until the police get here," the Cockney informed him outside the owner's suite. "She's quite safe—she won't be able to escape through the window."

"I'll send someone up to relieve you in half an hour."

Rex returned to the drawing room, aggrieved that his mother's oldest friend had resorted to murder and dragged an impressionable young girl into her schemes. Clearly, Mrs. Smithings was *non compos mentis*. He would testify to that fact in court and hopefully her mental state would be taken into consideration.

What would happen to Rosie was another matter.

———

Now that the veil of suspicion had been lifted from the rest of the residents, they began to relax.

"How long until the police get here?" Yvette asked from the loveseat. "I want to go home."

"Not me," Anthony said, having left Patrick in charge of Rosie. "I'm going to write a book. Patrick can do the illustrations. Rex, when did you start to suspect Rosie and Mrs. Smithings?" he questioned in reporter-like fashion.

"Once I realized Ms. Greenbaum's death was linked to the manuscript, my line of enquiry regarding Dahlia Smithings took on a domino effect. I just couldn't figure out how she returned to the kitchen unseen the night of Miriam's murder until Clifford showed me the covered path between the yew hedges."

"Reckon eh did show 'im," Clifford informed the gathering.

"My suspicions were reinforced by the fire in Lawdry's room. I told Mrs. Smithings yesterday afternoon that the police would be here today, and this must have prompted her to take action."

"And Rosie?" Anthony asked.

"Aye, well, Mrs. Smithings couldn't have acted alone. At first I thought Sandy Bellows had assisted her." Rex smiled apologetically at the cook. "She made the tarts, had a flimsy alibi for Ms. Greenbaum's murder, and was physically capable of smothering Wanda Martyr. But if Rosie had Mrs. Smithings' key, and Rosie's key was in Wanda's drawer, how would she have got in—unless there was a fourth key Mrs. Smithings hadn't told me about?"

Anthony nodded thoughtfully. "Possible."

"Anything was possible at that point," Rex agreed. "And I admit to being taken in by Rosie's act of wide-eyed innocence. But then, the generosity of the will was just too big to ignore. Why would Mrs. Smithings leave everything to a girl who'd been in her employment for eighteen months? There had to be a special bond between them. This train of thought was corroborated by Mrs. Bellows when she described how Rosie's twin had perished in the London bombings last year. I played a little trick on the cook at the same time by presenting her with the jar of cyanide and asking her to taste some tea, which I said contained a substance from that jar.

She passed with flying colours, and I was able to eliminate her as a suspect."

Mrs. Bellows stared at him in indignation. "Well, aren't you a devious one!"

"As I said before, Mrs. Bellows: 'Desperate times call for desperate measures.' I heard that from Mrs. Smithings the day I arrived, though I had no idea then what she was referring to."

"So, after that you concentrated on the Rosie theory," Anthony prompted.

Rex reached for Patrick's pad and showed Anthony the sketch. "Once I saw there was a single plate by the coffeepot, Rosie stood out as the obvious suspect. Mrs. Smithings devised the original plan and Rosie executed it—but it went awry. Rosie, feeling guilt over Lawdry's death, somewhat superstitiously left the last window of her advent calendar unopened. And then there was her little drama in the kitchen this morning when she tried to distract me from the truth by shifting blame onto Clifford."

At that moment, a blood-curdling scream rang out from the top of the stairs.

"Mercy," Mrs. Bellows cried, rushing from the room while the guests followed to the foot of the stairwell, none of them willing to proceed any farther. "That sounded like Mrs. Smithings. Whatever can be the matter?"

As she started up the stairs, Charley appeared on the landing. "Mrs. Smithings killed herself with a dagger. I rushed in when I heard the scream, but I was too late. There's blood everywhere."

"Hari-kari," Anthony muttered.

"I suppose we should have kept a suicide watch on her," Rex said with remorse. "I should have known she'd try something like this. If it's the Nepalese dagger from her office, she must have taken it upstairs at some point and been planning to use it."

Mrs. Bellows shook her head sadly. "This is the way she wanted to go in any case. She never wanted to end up in a home, let alone an institution like prison."

"Now Rosie will inherit the hotel," Yvette said.

"Not necessarily. The will may be deemed void if proven to have been drawn up as an inducement to commit an illegal act."

"Mrs. Smithings was genuinely fond of Rosie," the cook pointed out. "She could've written the will before she hatched the plot to murder the American guest."

"The jury might be sympathetic about Rosie losing her twin sister," Charley ventured.

"They might, were it not for Wanda's murder."

"Well, that's that, then," Mrs. Bellows said. "I suppose I'm out of a job. I'll still serve Christmas dinner, of course. I hope it's all right if me and Clifford join you."

"I'm sure I speak for everyone when I say it'll be our pleasure," Rex replied.

"Did you really have no idea what was going on?" Charley asked the cook.

"I wasn't here all the time before the snow started. And the last couple of days, I've been too busy to notice everything."

The doorbell chimed at that moment, and the people in the foyer froze in a stupor. Most of them had not seen a new face in days. Rex had almost forgotten about the police. "Well, I suppose we had better let them in," he said.

Grumbling, Clifford rose from his chair. "I'll get it. There be no peace around 'ere. This be the most 'orrible Christmas ever."

Rex gathered his notes and followed him to the front door.

"Merry Christmas, all," announced a man in a fluorescent yellow police parka, followed by a similarly dressed cop in a tall bobby hat. "Inspector Richard Driscoll at your service. This here is Sergeant Graeme Horne."

"Rex Graves, QC." Rex held out his hand while a team of black uniformed police filed past them, tracking slush across the parquet floor. "I spoke with you on the phone yesterday," he told the inspector. "The co-murderer is locked in the office." He indicated the door. "She and Mrs. Smithings concocted the first murder between them. I've written up a report."

"Right-oh. Three stiffs, wasn't it?"

"Four. Three murders—albeit, one accidental—and a suicide." Rex gave the inspector the master key and explained where the bodies were to be found.

"The coroner's right behind me, so we'll get cracking. As soon as we get all your statements, you can be on your way."

"We're staying for Christmas dinner to pay our respects to the departed. Mrs. Bellows here has been basting since daybreak. Turkey with chestnuts and brandy pudding."

The police officer chuckled. "Gluttons for punishment, the lot of you," he said, making his way through the hall.

After a quiet word with Rex, Helen followed the coroner upstairs. Mrs. Bellows headed for the kitchen. Rex ushered the rest of the residents back into the drawing room while the police conducted their business. He watched through the doors as the Forensic Science Service passed to and fro in white coveralls.

"What was the old lady hoping to achieve by bumping off Miriam Greenbaum and destroying the manuscript?" Patrick asked, returning from guard duty now that the police had arrived.

"It was a personal crusade to impede the Bush propaganda," Anthony said. "The murder was politically motivated."

"She was off her trolley," was Charley's comment. Reclining on the loveseat, he put his feet up on Yvette's lap.

"I feel sorry for her," she said.

"You feel sorry for everybody."

Clifford twisted his cap in his hands. "Now she be dead."

Rex could not conceive of his mother's reaction to the news. He would wait to tell her until she returned from visiting her sick friend in Perth—she had enough on her plate for now.

Some time later, Helen stepped into the room. "Well, I should be going."

"Aren't you staying for Christmas dinner?" Yvette asked.

"I spoke to the medical examiner. They'll be ready to take Wanda to the morgue soon. I thought I'd go with her."

"How awful for you." Yvette pushed Charley's feet off her lap and got up to embrace Helen.

"This is my number and address in Derby," Helen told her. "Do write."

"We will."

"Patrick, Anthony." Helen hugged them both. "I wish we could have met under happier circumstances."

"We'd love to keep in touch," Anthony said. "Here's our card."

Helen nodded and with a glance at Rex, sidled into the hallway.

"I have a big lump in my throat," he said, following her to the front door.

"Not bigger than mine."

"I'm going to miss you."

"Stop it." Pressing her lips together, she stood staring at her boots.

"Shall I come with you to the morgue?"

Helen shook her head, ensconced in the blue woolen bonnet. "No need. I'll head on home afterwards. The main roads should be clear. I only hope my car starts."

"I asked Clifford to clear the snow off your windscreen."

Helen winced. "Now I know I'm in trouble."

"Let me take your suitcase."

"You really should put on a coat. You'll freeze."

Rex picked up the case and followed her out the door and down the newly shoveled path to the parking area off the driveway. She popped open the trunk of a Renault and tucked in her bags, leaving space for the suitcase. Rex closed the hatch while she tried to start the car. The engine neighed slowly on the first two attempts and then caught.

Leaving the car idling, she got out and turned to Rex. "So this is goodbye," she said with a trembling smile.

"I canna stand goodbye, so 'tis farewell."

Helen fell onto his chest, sobbing against his sweater. "I'm sorry," she faltered. "I meant to be so brave."

"Ah, lassie." He cupped her bonnet in one hand and held her against him while she regained control of herself.

"It's just been too much, what with Wanda and everything," she explained.

"I know." Holding her elbow, he assisted her back into the car.

She pulled the door closed and buzzed down the window. Her smudged mascara brought out the pale blue of her eyes. "I best get going. The coroner's van is pulling out."

Turning around, he saw the van inch its way toward them through the grooves in the snow. As it passed, he tapped on the roof of the car, and Helen put it into gear. He stood back and watched her leave. The exhaust chugged out gray plumes in the cold air, which penetrated his sweater like needles of ice.

"Stay in touch," he called out, forming a megaphone with his numb hands.

Helen waved back from the car.

"Promise!"

He could not hear her reply. The car turned out of the gates. His hands fell to his sides, a mass of emotions writhing in the pit of his stomach. Would he ever see her again?

It was up to him. He held the cards—until she met someone else, or resigned herself to Clive. Rex felt a twinge of panic. He had lost too many people.

SEVENTEEN

"Chestnuts roasting on an open fire," Patrick sang out as he stalked toward the fireplace with a handful of mahogany-shelled nuts. "Bellows gave me these and chased me out of the kitchen. Said she could manage quite well with Clifford and that dinner would be on the table in half an hour. She apologizes for the delay due to the police investigation."

Rex sat back in his armchair with a tumbler of vintage port in one hand and his pipe in the other. The dog scrambled into his lap and rested its black muzzle on its forepaws. He patted its wiry coat, remembering how he'd brought it to Swanmere Manor only three days before—so much had happened in that short time.

"*Acta est fabula,*" he said, speaking before he knew it.

"You what?" Charley asked.

"It's Latin," Patrick said.

"The drama has been acted out," Rex translated.

"It certainly has." Anthony, legs crossed in his chair by the fire, held up his glass of port as if to admire the amber lights reflecting off the flames. "To absent acquaintances," he toasted.

"To absent acquaintances," Rex repeated solemnly. "Patrick, when are you going to let me see that drawing you did of me?" he asked after observing several moments of silence.

The young man picked the sketchpad off the sofa and showed him the portrait.

"It makes me look superior." Though Rex thought it was actually quite flattering. "Can you add a wee bit of colour? Mrs. Wilcox might like to have it." He wondered again how she would be spending Christmas in Iraq.

"On one condition," Patrick said.

"What's that?"

"That you let me change the colour of that cravat."

"What's wrong with it?"

"It's orange." Patrick made a disparaging face. "Aubergine would bring out the green of your eyes more and would go better with your brown corduroy suit."

"Corduroy!" Anthony lamented.

"Oh, verra well then."

"So what's this about a Mrs. Wilcox?" Charley asked.

Yvette nudged him. "It's rude to ask questions."

"He asked us all those questions. It's only right he should answer ours."

Rex ducked his chin, smiling. "Fair enough. What do you want to know?"

"About this Mrs. Wilcox, for starters."

"Anything but that. Thanks," he said, accepting the fire-cracked chestnut from Patrick's iron tongs.

He juggled it from one hand to the other. Once it was cool enough, he peeled off the shell and bit into the sweet meat. This, more than anything, encapsulated the taste of Christmas, he reflected. He dedicated a wistful thought to Helen who would be on the long drive north to Derbyshire by now. He thought about the swans on the lake, her bare feet on his heels, the kiss under the mistletoe …

"Cheer up, Rex, it's Christmas," Patrick murmured, intent on his drawing.

"Aye, so it is."

Rex fell into a reverie. So much for a peaceful Yuletide. On top of everything, he had witnessed the downfall of the indomitable Mrs. Smithings—disconcerting to realize that one of the bastions of his childhood had crumbled so ignobly … He wondered if she had subtly thrown him the challenge of solving the mystery. He wouldn't put it past her. She may even have hoped he would solve it. Her voice echoed in his head: *Reginald, you always were one step ahead of everybody else.*

If you enjoyed *Christmas is Murder*, read on for an excerpt
from the next Rex Graves Mystery

Murder in the Raw

Coming soon from Midnight Ink

ST. MARTIN,
FRENCH WEST INDIES
TESTIMONY OF DAVID WEEKS

IT IS INCREDIBLE THAT Sabine Durand is dead. She was the essence of our group, the lingering perfume, if you will. Whenever I evoke Saint Martin, it is always Sabine I conjure up in my memory.

I often saw her walking at dusk along the shore, always alone. Our beach cabana is the last of eight before the promontory of rocks begins on the eastern side. She would have had to climb those rocks to get to the strand of beach beyond, but she was agile enough, I suppose. In any case, there was no other access except by boat. People sometimes dock their catamarans on that side, but since you can sunbathe nude all along La Plage d'Azur, there really isn't any point in going over there unless you want to "do it" au nature. People, after all, pay big money to be seen in the buff at La Plage.

We've been coming to Saint Martin for ten years now. You end up synchronizing your holiday with other couples. It's always the same crowd in July: Paul and Elizabeth Winslow, Dick and Penny Irving, the O'Sullivans, the von Muellers, the Farleys . . . Duke Farley has been bringing his new wife, Pam, the last couple of years, so I suppose it's not exactly the same crowd as before. Brooklyn Chalmers brought a girlfriend two years ago, but not this time around. And, of course, Vernon and Sabine. July is by far and away the best time. August is Swingers' Month and come September you run into hurricane season.

I don't know whether we'll return next year. It won't be the same without Sabine, and I doubt Vernon will come back, poor fellow. He must feel dreadfully guilty. After all, he never accompanied his wife on her walks, though I think she preferred it that way. She was remote and mysterious. I think that was part of the allure. She drew people like moths to a candle. You wanted to protect her from singeing her wings, sort of thing. Well, the others will say the same, I'm sure.

Sabine always wore the diaphanous white pareo on her walks. She would have taken it off before she went for a swim, which would explain why part of it was found by the rocks. But she wouldn't have gone for a dip right before dinner. I don't go for the shark theory—she would have known better than to go swimming at dusk. Then again, she never was the sort of person to do what you'd expect. More likely a stalker was involved; actresses often attract that sort.

It must have been just after six PM on Tuesday 10th when I saw her for the last time on her walk. We usually all meet at seven for drinks at The Cockatoo. My wife and I sometimes escorted Sabine to the restaurant on her way back, but it was Paul Winslow's birthday, and we didn't want to be late, so we left our cabana in good time. We never saw Sabine again.

Those are my recollections of the night in question.

Signed,

David Weeks

ACKNOWLEDGMENTS

My thanks to my husband, mother-in-law, and friend Andrée for their encouragement and helpful comments upon reading the manuscript, and also to my partner-in-crime Fred, who provides feline company through hours of solitude at the computer.

ABOUT THE AUTHOR

Born in Bloomington, Indiana, and now residing permanently in Florida, C. S. Challinor was educated in Scotland and England, and holds a joint honors degree in Latin and French from the University of Kent, Canterbury, as well as a diploma in Russian from the Pushkin Institute in Moscow. Her professional background is in Florida real estate. She has traveled extensively and enjoys discovering new territory for her novels.

Fifteen percent of royalty proceeds for this book will go to Soldiers' Angels, a non-profit organization that helps rehabilitate United States veterans wounded in Afghanistan and Iraq.

Visit C.S. Challinor on the web at www.rexgraves.com.

WWW.MIDNIGHTINKBOOKS.COM

From the gritty streets of New York City to sacred tombs in the Middle East, it's always midnight somewhere. Join us online at any hour for fresh new voices in mystery fiction.

At midnightinkbooks.com you'll also find our author blog, new and upcoming books, events, book club questions, excerpts, mystery resources, and more.

MIDNIGHT INK ORDERING INFORMATION

Order Online:
• Visit our website www.midnightinkbooks.com, select your books, and order them on our secure server.

Order by Phone:
• Call toll-free within the U.S. and Canada at
  1-888-NITE-INK (1-888-648-3465)
• We accept VISA, MasterCard, and American Express

Order by Mail:
Send the full price of your order (MN residents add 6.5% sales tax) in U.S. funds, plus postage & handling to:

> Midnight Ink
> 2143 Wooddale Drive
> Woodbury, MN 55125-2989

Postage & Handling:
Standard (U.S., Mexico, and Canada). If your order is:
> $24.99 and under, add $3.00
> $25.00 and over, FREE STANDARD SHIPPING

AK, HI, PR: $15.00 for one book plus $1.00 for each additional book.

International Orders (airmail only):
> $16.00 for one book plus $3.00 for each additional book

Orders are processed within 2 business days. Please allow for normal shipping time. Postage and handling rates subject to change.